D1088876

BATMAN

THE BRAVE AND THE BOLD

THE ALL NEW!

STONE ARCH BOOKS
a capstone imprint

STONE ARCH BOOKS™

Published in 2015 by Stone Arch Books
A Capstone Imprint
1710 Roe Crest Drive
North Mankato, MN 56003
www.capstonepub.com

Originally published by DC Comics in the U.S. in single magazine form as The All-New Batman: The Brave and the Bold #1.
Original U.S. Editor: Scott Peterson

Library of Congress Cataloging-in-Publication Data

Fisch, Sholly, author.
Bottle of the planets / Sholly Fisch, writer ; Rick Burchett, penciller ; Dan Davis, inker ; Wildstorm FX, colorist.
pages cm. -- [The all-new Batman: the brave and the bold ; 1]
"Originally published by DC Comics in the U.S. in single magazine form as The All-New Batman: The Brave and the Bold #1."
"Batman created by Bob Kane."

Summary: When Kandor is threatened by a plague of thefts, Superman and Batman shrink down to super-small size to unravel the mystery.

ISBN 978-1-4342-9658-0 [library binding]
1. Batman [Fictitious character]--Comic books, strips, etc. 2. Batman [Fictitious character]--Juvenile fiction. 3. Superman [Fictitious character]--Comic books, strips, etc. 4. Superman [Fictitious character]--Juvenile fiction. 5. Superheroes--Comic books, strips, etc. 6. Superheroes--Juvenile fiction. 7. Theft--Comic books, strips, etc. 8. Theft--Juvenile fiction. 9. Graphic novels. [1. Graphic novels. 2. Superheroes--Fiction. 3. Size--Fiction. 4. Stealing--Fiction.] I. Burchett, Rick, illustrator. II. Kane, Bob, creator. III. Title.

PZ7.7.F57Bo 2015
741.5'973--dc23

2014028250

STONE ARCH BOOKS
Ashley C. Andersen Zantop Publisher
Michael Dahl Editorial Director
Eliza Leahy Editor
Heather Kindseth Creative Director
Bob Lentz Art Director
Peggie Carley Designer
Katy LaVigne Production Specialist

Printed in China by Nordica.
0914/CA21401510
092014 008470NORD515

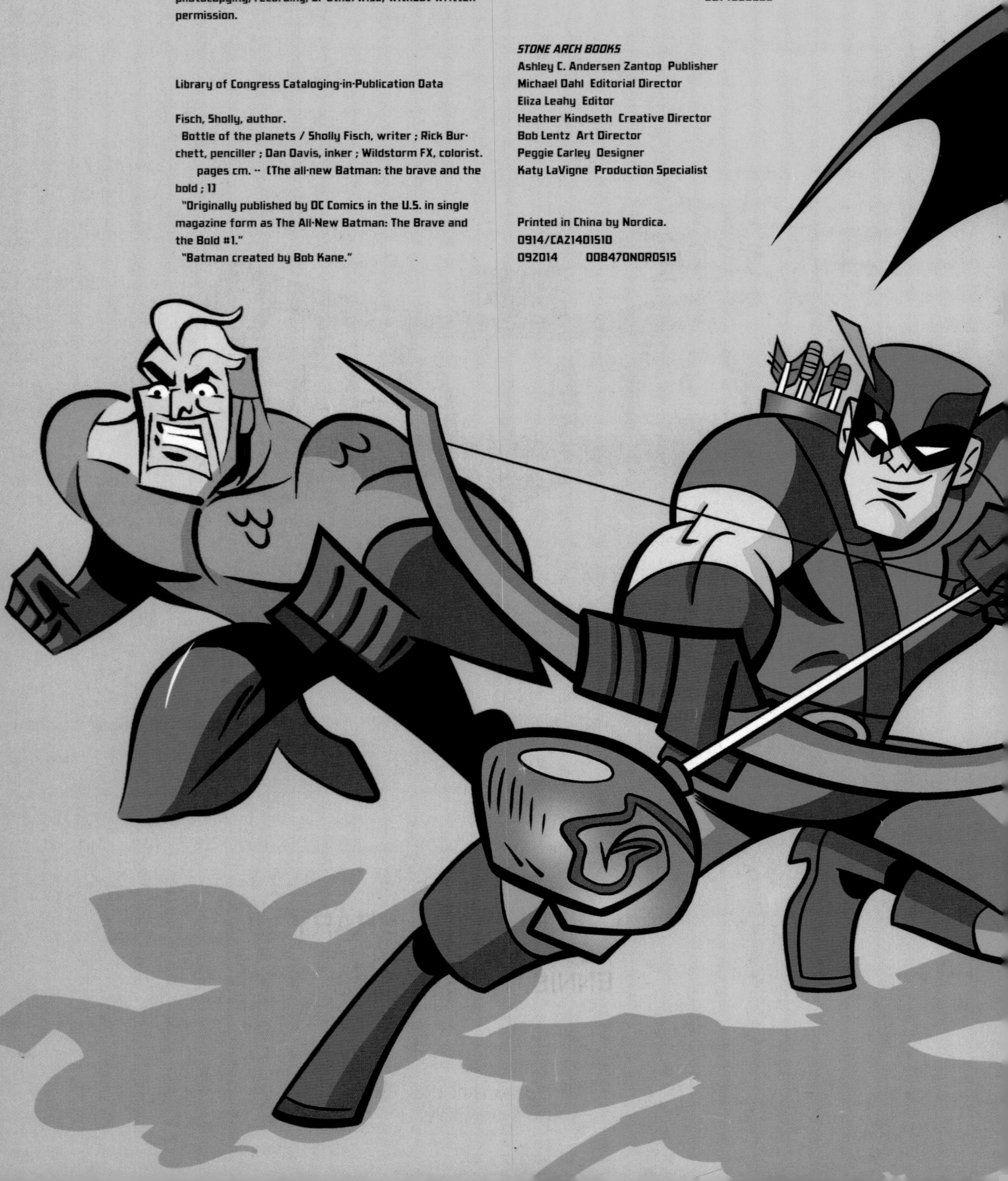

THE ALL NEW!

BATMAN

THE BRAVE AND THE BOLD

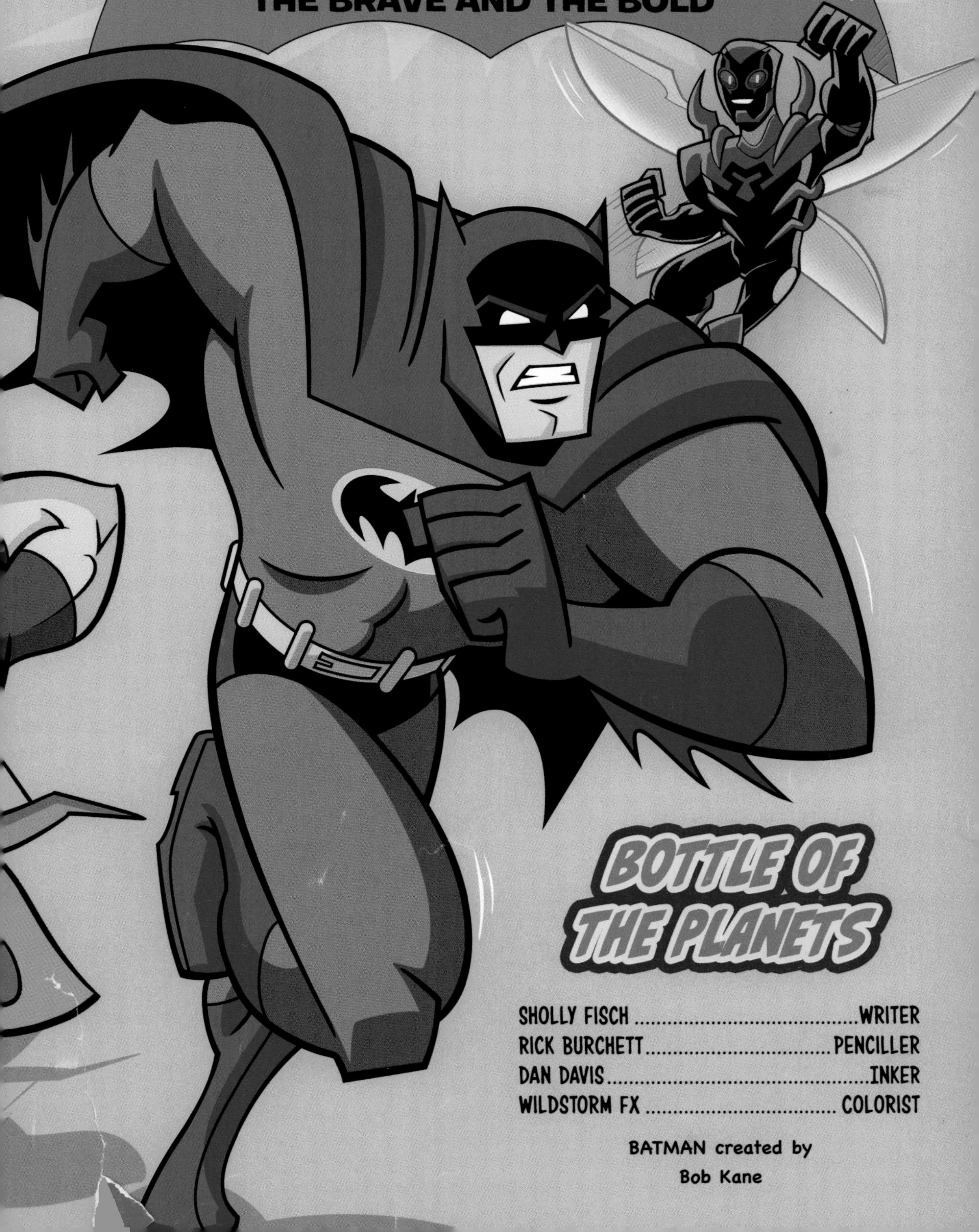

BOTTLE OF THE PLANETS

SHOLLY FISCH .... WRITER
RICK BURCHETT .... PENCILLER
DAN DAVIS .... INKER
WILDSTORM FX .... COLORIST

BATMAN created by
Bob Kane

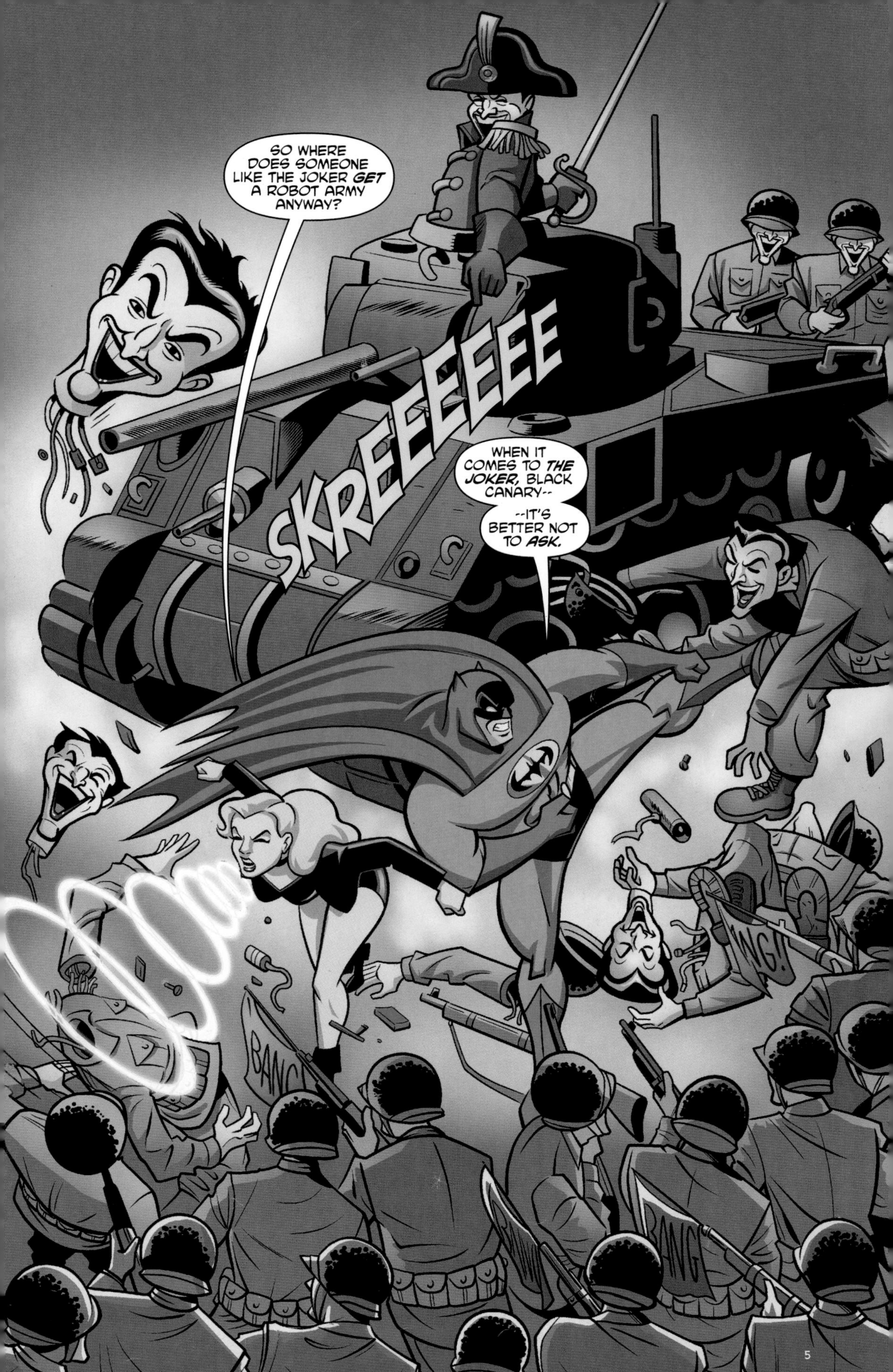
SO WHERE DOES SOMEONE LIKE THE JOKER GET A ROBOT ARMY ANYWAY?
SKREEEEEEE
WHEN IT COMES TO THE JOKER, BLACK CANARY--
--IT'S BETTER NOT TO ASK.
BANG
BANG
BANG

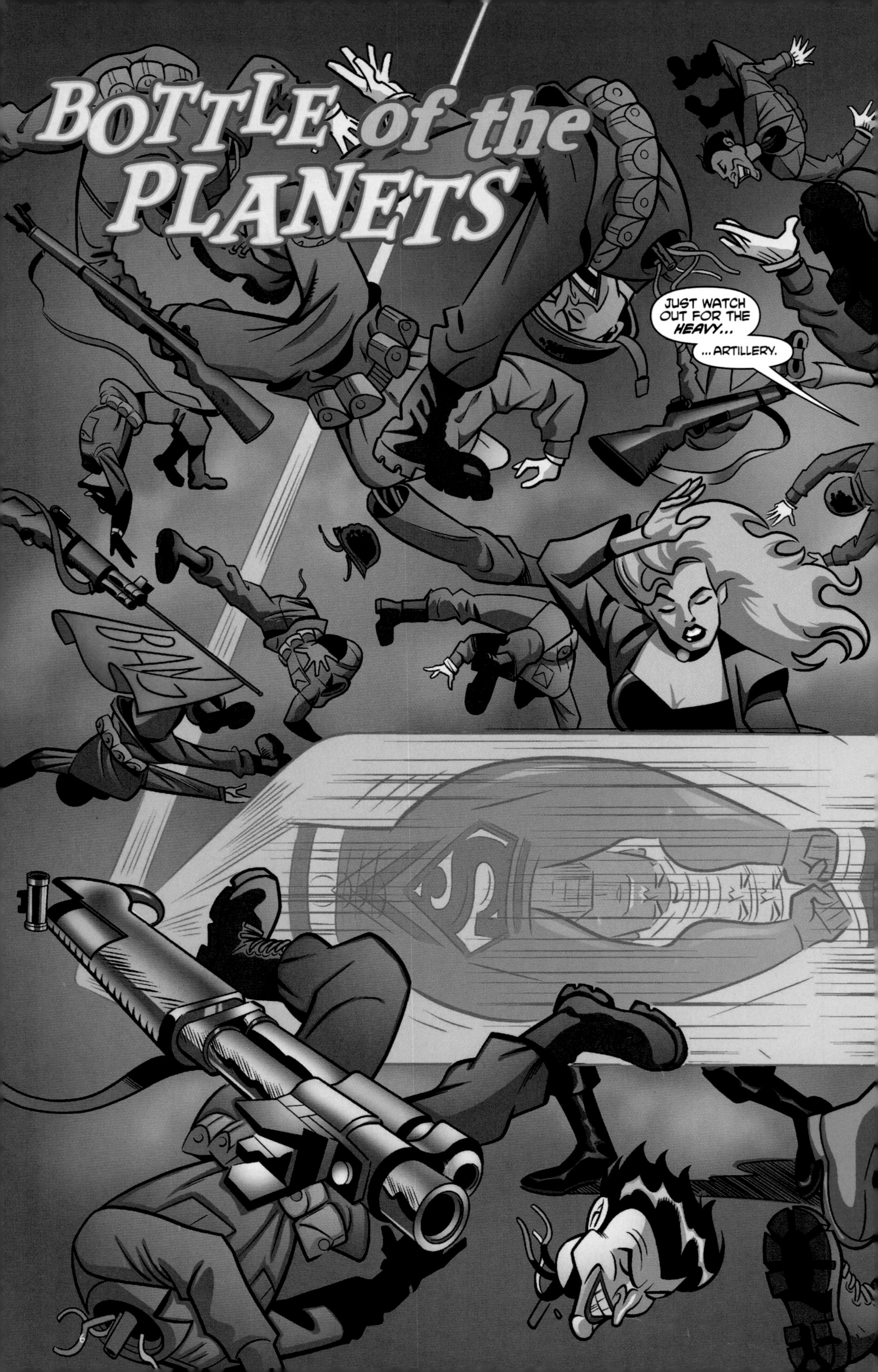
BOTTLE of the PLANETS
JUST WATCH OUT FOR THE HEAVY...
...ARTILLERY.

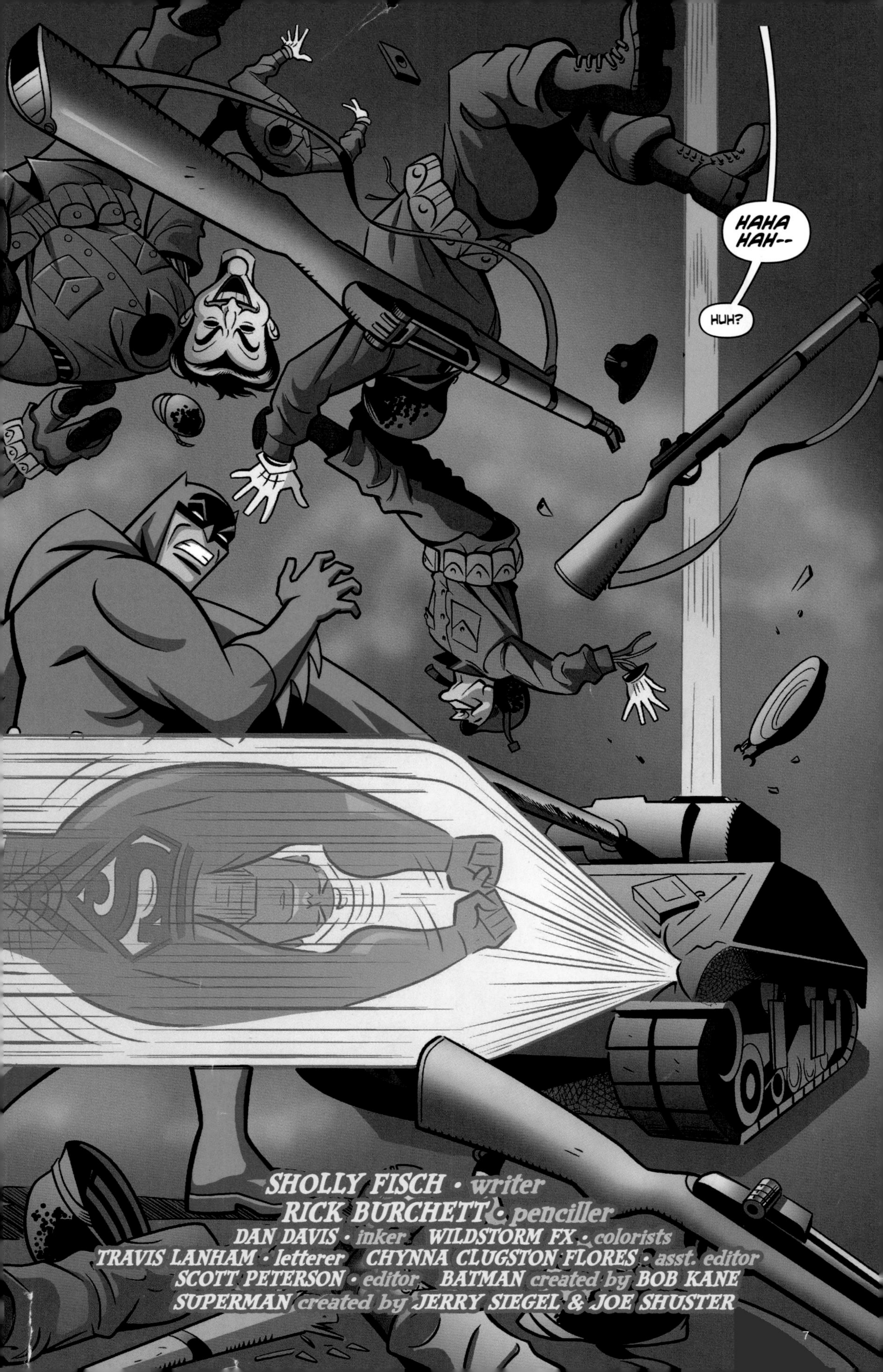
HAHA HAH--
HUH?
SHOLLY FISCH • writer
RICK BURCHETT • penciller
DAN DAVIS • inker WILDSTORM FX • colorists
TRAVIS LANHAM • letterer CHYNNA CLUGSTON FLORES • asst. editor
SCOTT PETERSON • editor BATMAN created by BOB KANE
SUPERMAN created by JERRY SIEGEL & JOE SHUSTER

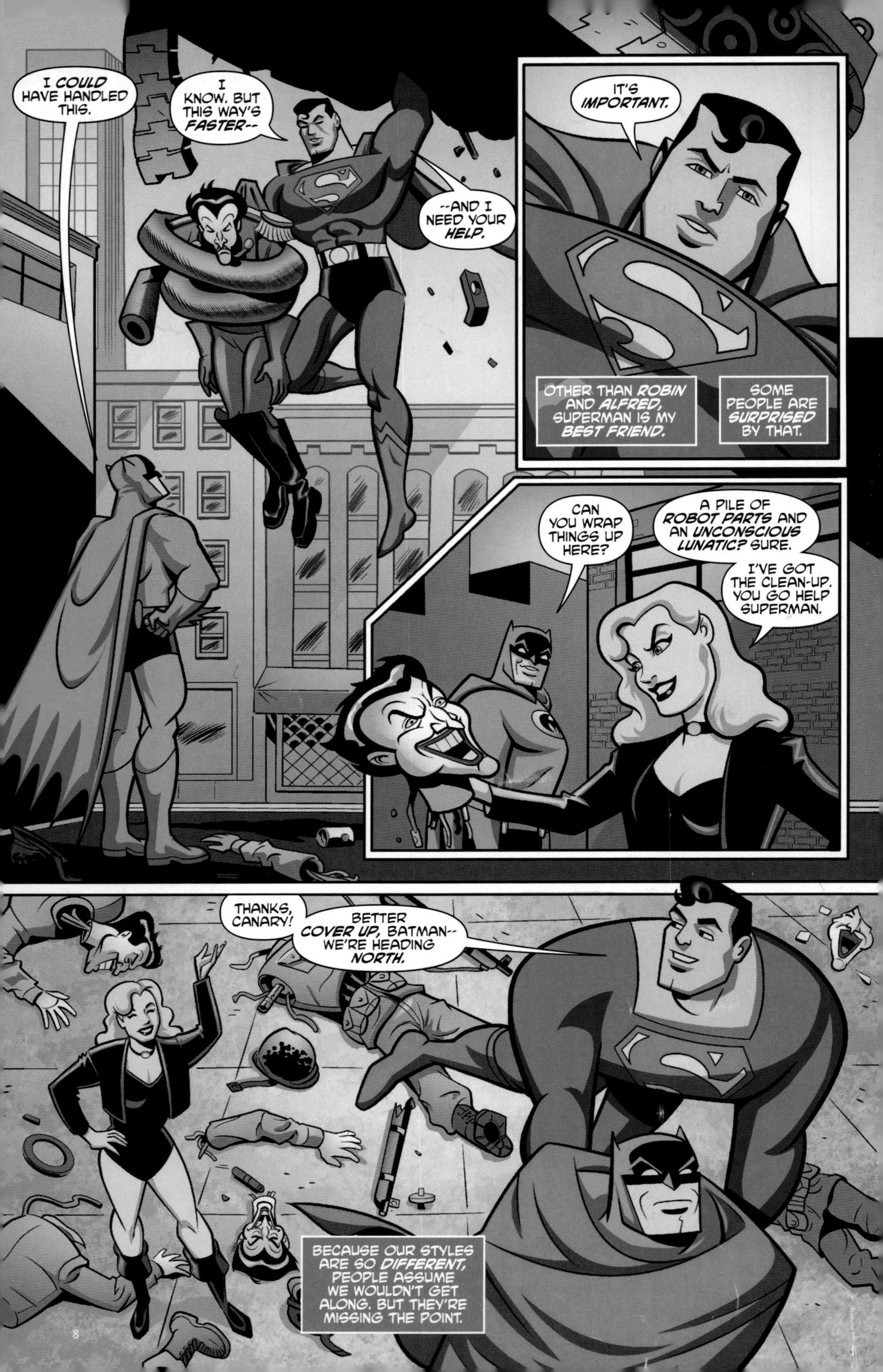
I COULD HAVE HANDLED THIS.
I KNOW. BUT THIS WAY'S FASTER--
--AND I NEED YOUR HELP.
IT'S IMPORTANT.
OTHER THAN ROBIN AND ALFRED, SUPERMAN IS MY BEST FRIEND.
SOME PEOPLE ARE SURPRISED BY THAT.
CAN YOU WRAP THINGS UP HERE?
A PILE OF ROBOT PARTS AND AN UNCONSCIOUS LUNATIC? SURE.
I'VE GOT THE CLEAN-UP. YOU GO HELP SUPERMAN.
THANKS, CANARY!
BETTER COVER UP, BATMAN-- WE'RE HEADING NORTH.
BECAUSE OUR STYLES ARE SO DIFFERENT, PEOPLE ASSUME WE WOULDN'T GET ALONG. BUT THEY'RE MISSING THE POINT.

WHEN I'M WITH SOMEONE LIKE GREEN ARROW, WE'RE SO SIMILAR THAT WE FEEL LIKE WE HAVE TO COMPETE.
I COULD USE YOUR DETECTIVE SKILLS. I GOT A DISTRESS CALL ABOUT A RASH OF MYSTERIOUS THEFTS--
BUT SUPERMAN AND I HAVE DIFFERENT STRENGTHS.
--FROM HERE, INSIDE THE BOTTLE CITY OF KANDOR!
CAN'T THE LOCAL POLICE DEAL WITH IT?
WE COMPLEMENT EACH OTHER.
KANDOR'S A HIGHLY ADVANCED KRYPTONIAN SOCIETY, SHRUNK DOWN IN A BOTTLE. THEY DON'T HAVE MUCH CRIME.
IN FACT, EVEN BEFORE KRYPTON EXPLODED, PEOPLE USED TO SAY MOST OF THE CRIME WAS COMMITTED BY AN UNKNOWN RACE OF INVISIBLE PEOPLE.
"INVISIBLE PEOPLE." RIGHT.
SO NO POLICE IN KANDOR.
NOT REALLY, ALTHOUGH THEY DO HAVE A MILITARY GUILD FOR DEFENSE.
AND NO SUPER-HEROES.
PRESENT COMPANY EXCEPTED.

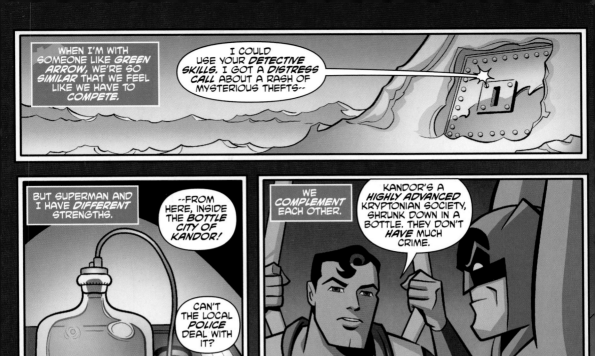

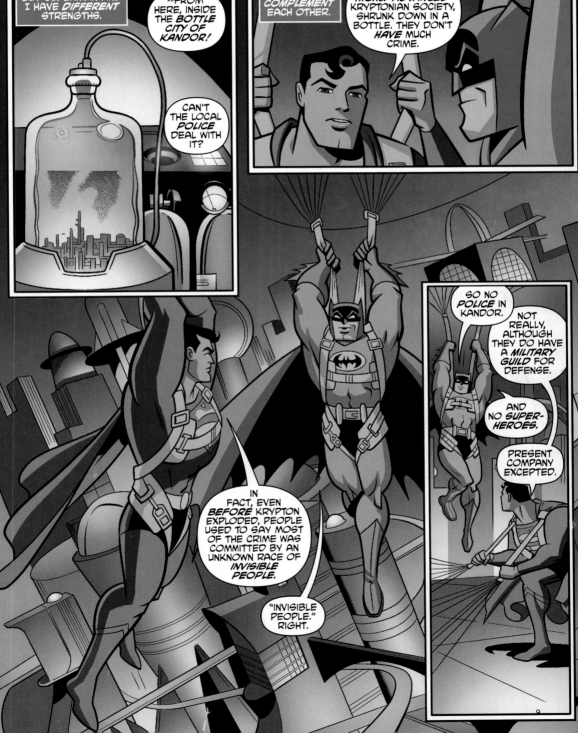

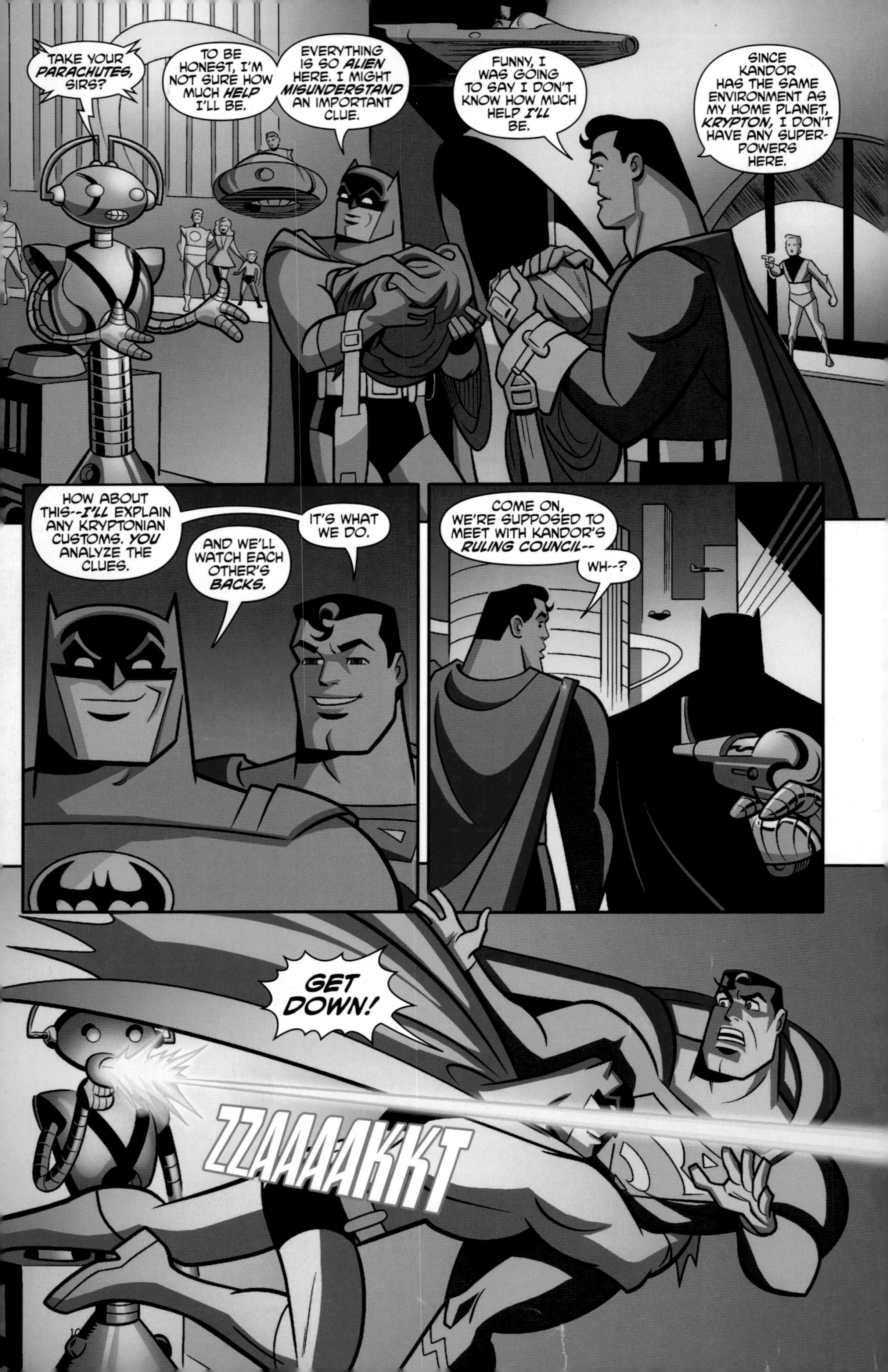
TAKE YOUR PARACHUTES, SIRS?
TO BE HONEST, I'M NOT SURE HOW MUCH HELP I'LL BE.
EVERYTHING IS SO ALIEN HERE. I MIGHT MISUNDERSTAND AN IMPORTANT CLUE.
FUNNY, I WAS GOING TO SAY I DON'T KNOW HOW MUCH HELP I'LL BE.
SINCE KANDOR HAS THE SAME ENVIRONMENT AS MY HOME PLANET, KRYPTON, I DON'T HAVE ANY SUPER-POWERS HERE.
HOW ABOUT THIS--I'LL EXPLAIN ANY KRYPTONIAN CUSTOMS. YOU ANALYZE THE CLUES.
IT'S WHAT WE DO.
AND WE'LL WATCH EACH OTHER'S BACKS.
COME ON, WE'RE SUPPOSED TO MEET WITH KANDOR'S RULING COUNCIL--
WH--?
GET DOWN!
ZZAAAAKKT

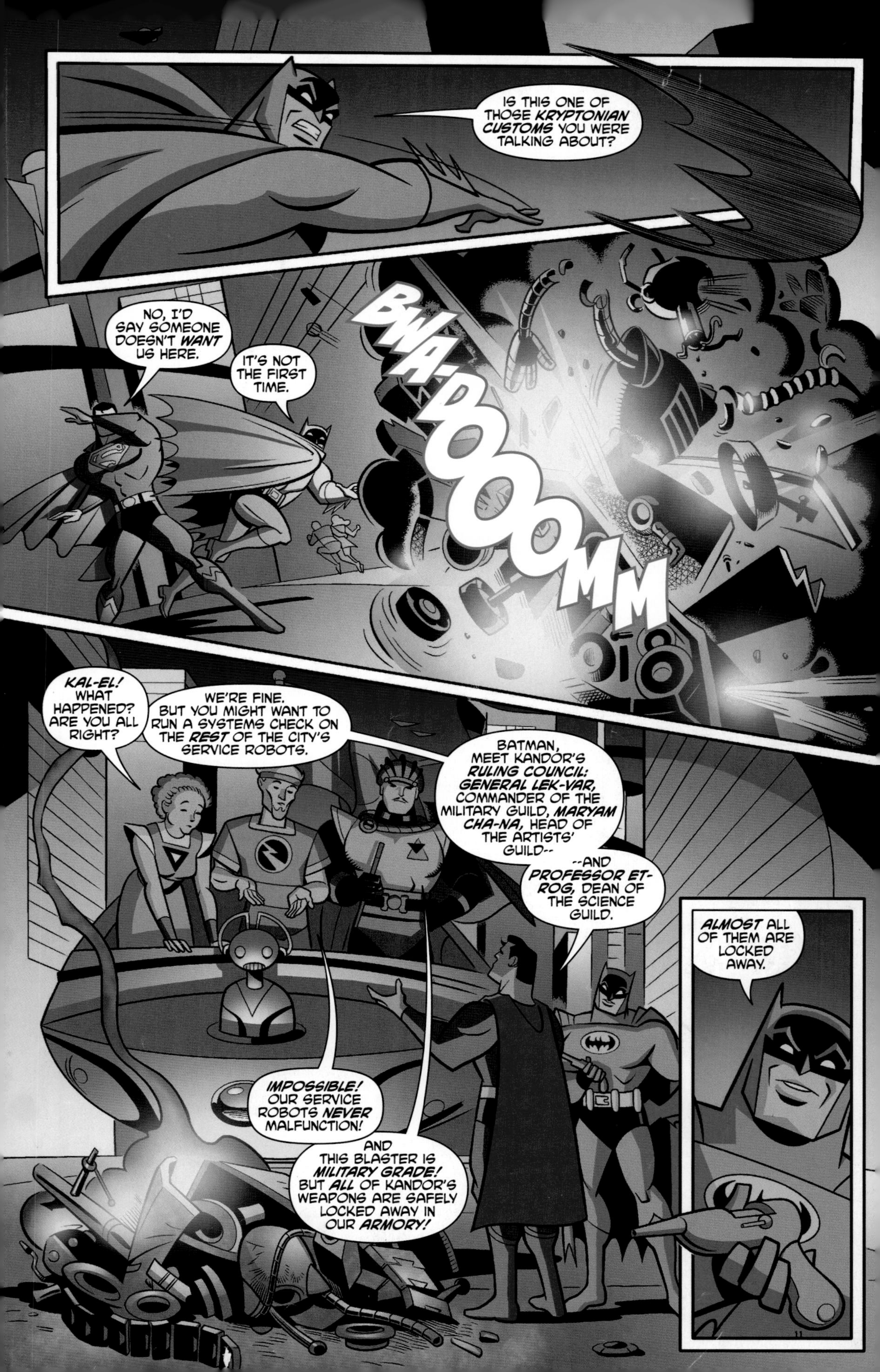

IS THIS ONE OF THOSE *KRYPTONIAN CUSTOMS* YOU WERE TALKING ABOUT?
NO, I'D SAY SOMEONE DOESN'T *WANT* US HERE.
IT'S NOT THE FIRST TIME.
BWA-DOOOOMM
KAL-EL! WHAT HAPPENED? ARE YOU ALL RIGHT?
WE'RE FINE. BUT YOU MIGHT WANT TO RUN A SYSTEMS CHECK ON THE *REST* OF THE CITY'S SERVICE ROBOTS.
BATMAN, MEET KANDOR'S *RULING COUNCIL: GENERAL LEK-VAR,* COMMANDER OF THE MILITARY GUILD, *MARYAM CHA-NA,* HEAD OF THE ARTISTS' GUILD--
--AND *PROFESSOR ET-ROG,* DEAN OF THE SCIENCE GUILD.
IMPOSSIBLE! OUR SERVICE ROBOTS *NEVER* MALFUNCTION!
AND THIS BLASTER IS *MILITARY GRADE!* BUT *ALL* OF KANDOR'S WEAPONS ARE SAFELY LOCKED AWAY IN OUR *ARMORY!*
ALMOST ALL OF THEM ARE LOCKED AWAY.

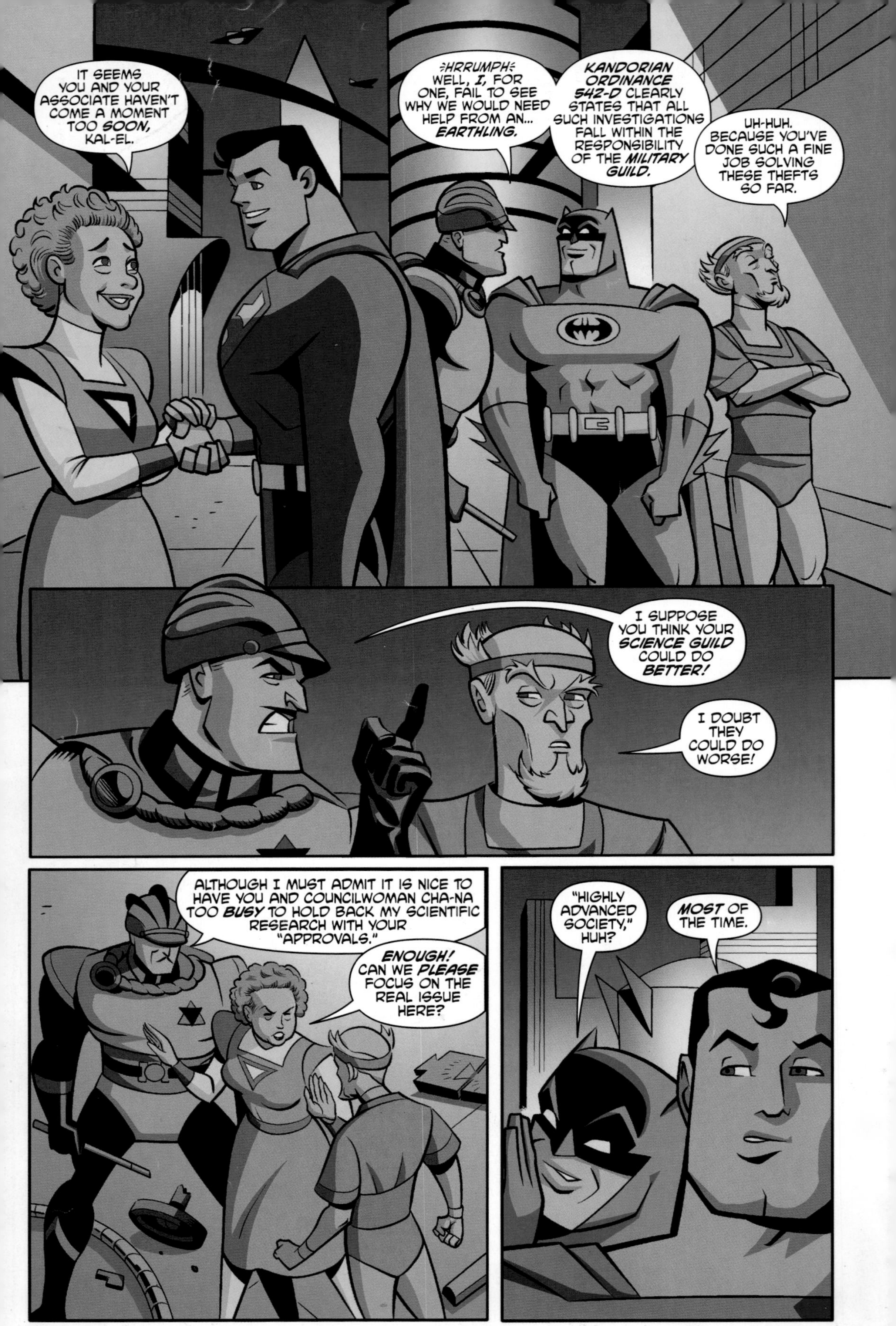
IT SEEMS YOU AND YOUR ASSOCIATE HAVEN'T COME A MOMENT TOO SOON, KAL-EL.
HRRUMPH WELL, I, FOR ONE, FAIL TO SEE WHY WE WOULD NEED HELP FROM AN... EARTHLING.
KANDORIAN ORDINANCE 542-D CLEARLY STATES THAT ALL SUCH INVESTIGATIONS FALL WITHIN THE RESPONSIBILITY OF THE MILITARY GUILD.
UH-HUH. BECAUSE YOU'VE DONE SUCH A FINE JOB SOLVING THESE THEFTS SO FAR.
I SUPPOSE YOU THINK YOUR SCIENCE GUILD COULD DO BETTER!
I DOUBT THEY COULD DO WORSE!
ALTHOUGH I MUST ADMIT IT IS NICE TO HAVE YOU AND COUNCILWOMAN CHA-NA TOO BUSY TO HOLD BACK MY SCIENTIFIC RESEARCH WITH YOUR "APPROVALS."
ENOUGH! CAN WE PLEASE FOCUS ON THE REAL ISSUE HERE?
"HIGHLY ADVANCED SOCIETY," HUH?
MOST OF THE TIME.

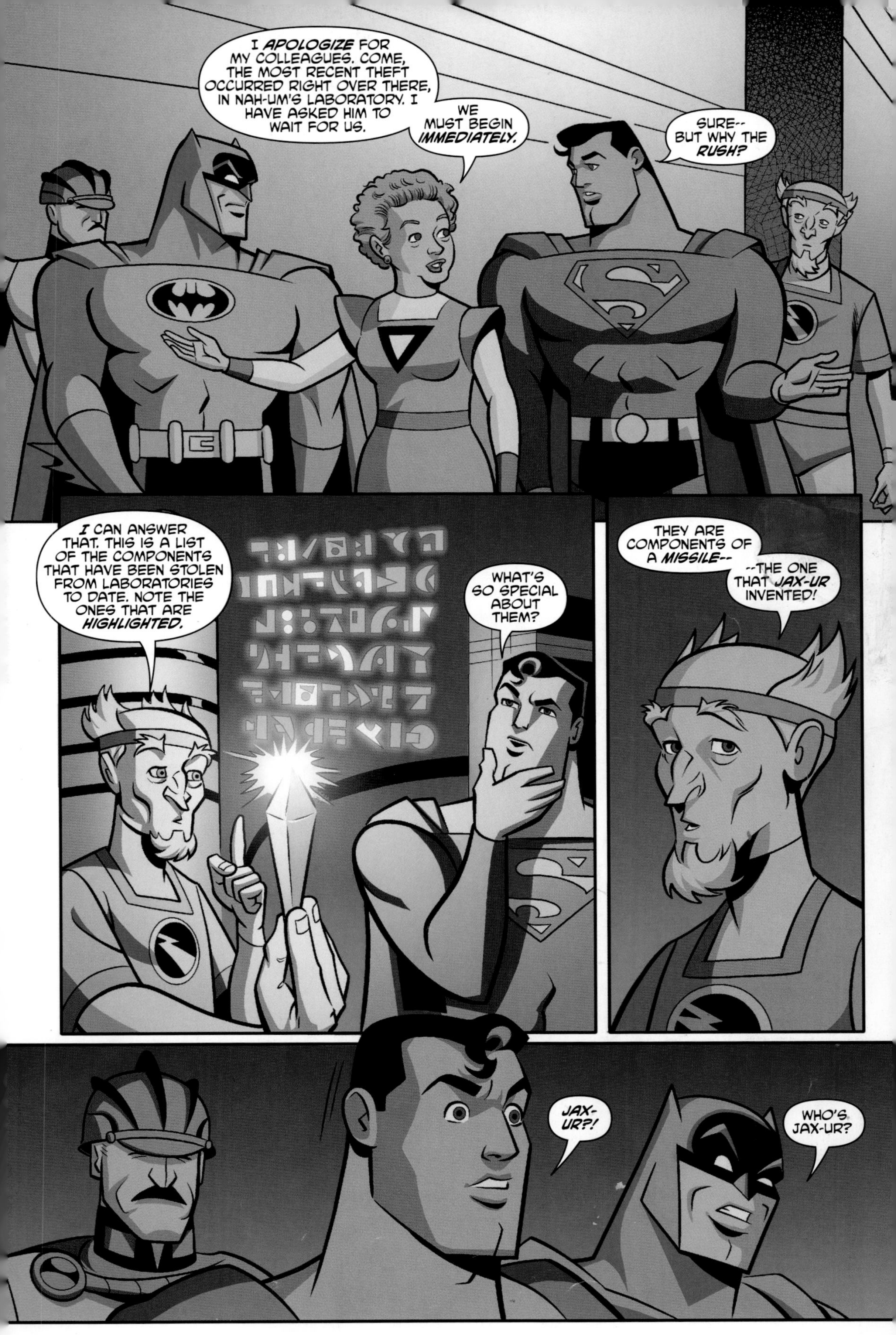
I APOLOGIZE FOR MY COLLEAGUES. COME, THE MOST RECENT THEFT OCCURRED RIGHT OVER THERE, IN NAH-UM'S LABORATORY. I HAVE ASKED HIM TO WAIT FOR US.
WE MUST BEGIN IMMEDIATELY.
SURE-- BUT WHY THE RUSH?
I CAN ANSWER THAT. THIS IS A LIST OF THE COMPONENTS THAT HAVE BEEN STOLEN FROM LABORATORIES TO DATE. NOTE THE ONES THAT ARE HIGHLIGHTED.
WHAT'S SO SPECIAL ABOUT THEM?
THEY ARE COMPONENTS OF A MISSILE--
--THE ONE THAT JAX-UR INVENTED!
JAX-UR?!
WHO'S JAX-UR?

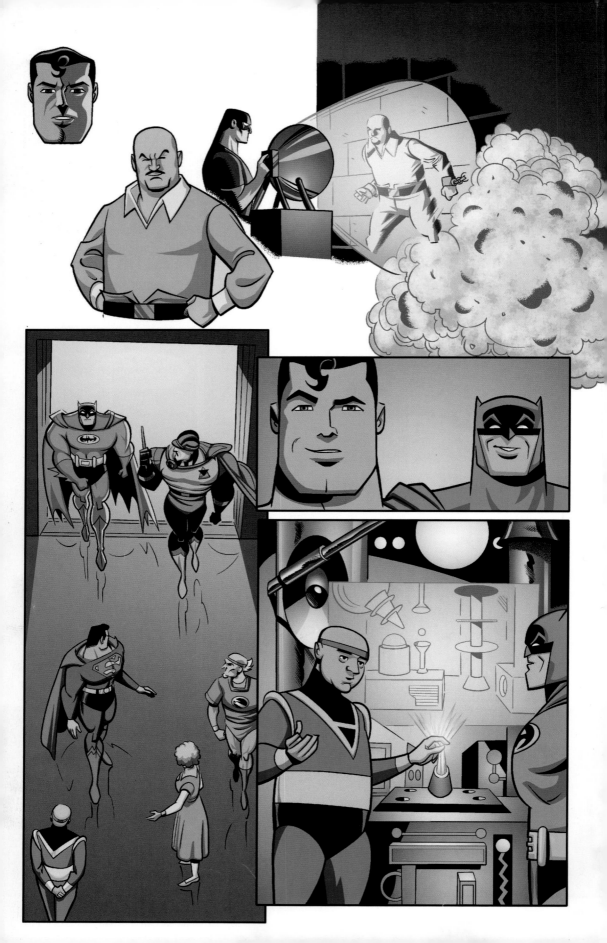

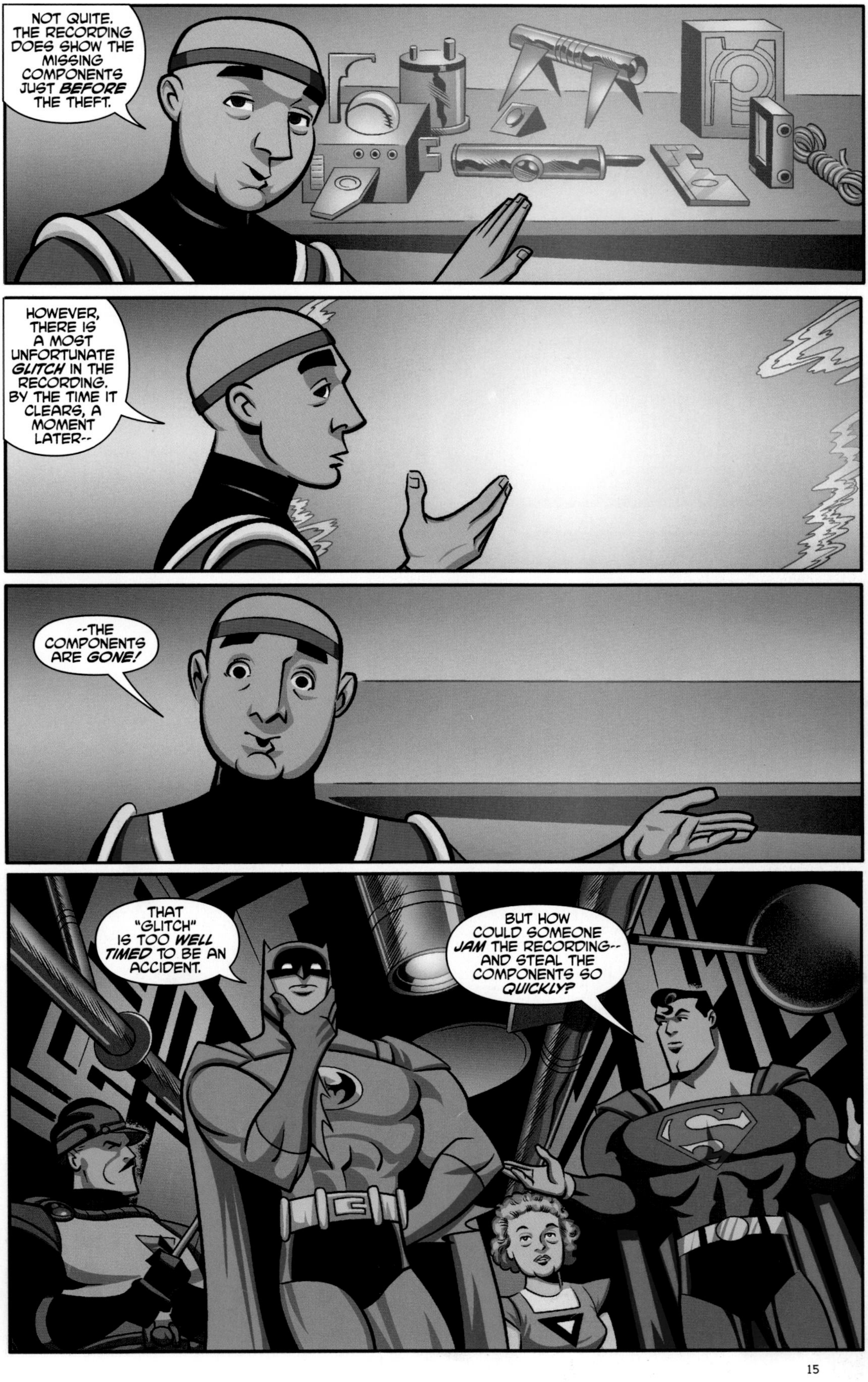
NOT QUITE. THE RECORDING DOES SHOW THE MISSING COMPONENTS JUST *BEFORE* THE THEFT.
HOWEVER, THERE IS A MOST UNFORTUNATE *GLITCH* IN THE RECORDING. BY THE TIME IT CLEARS, A MOMENT LATER--
--THE COMPONENTS ARE *GONE!*
THAT "GLITCH" IS TOO *WELL TIMED* TO BE AN ACCIDENT.
BUT HOW COULD SOMEONE *JAM* THE RECORDING--AND STEAL THE COMPONENTS SO *QUICKLY?*

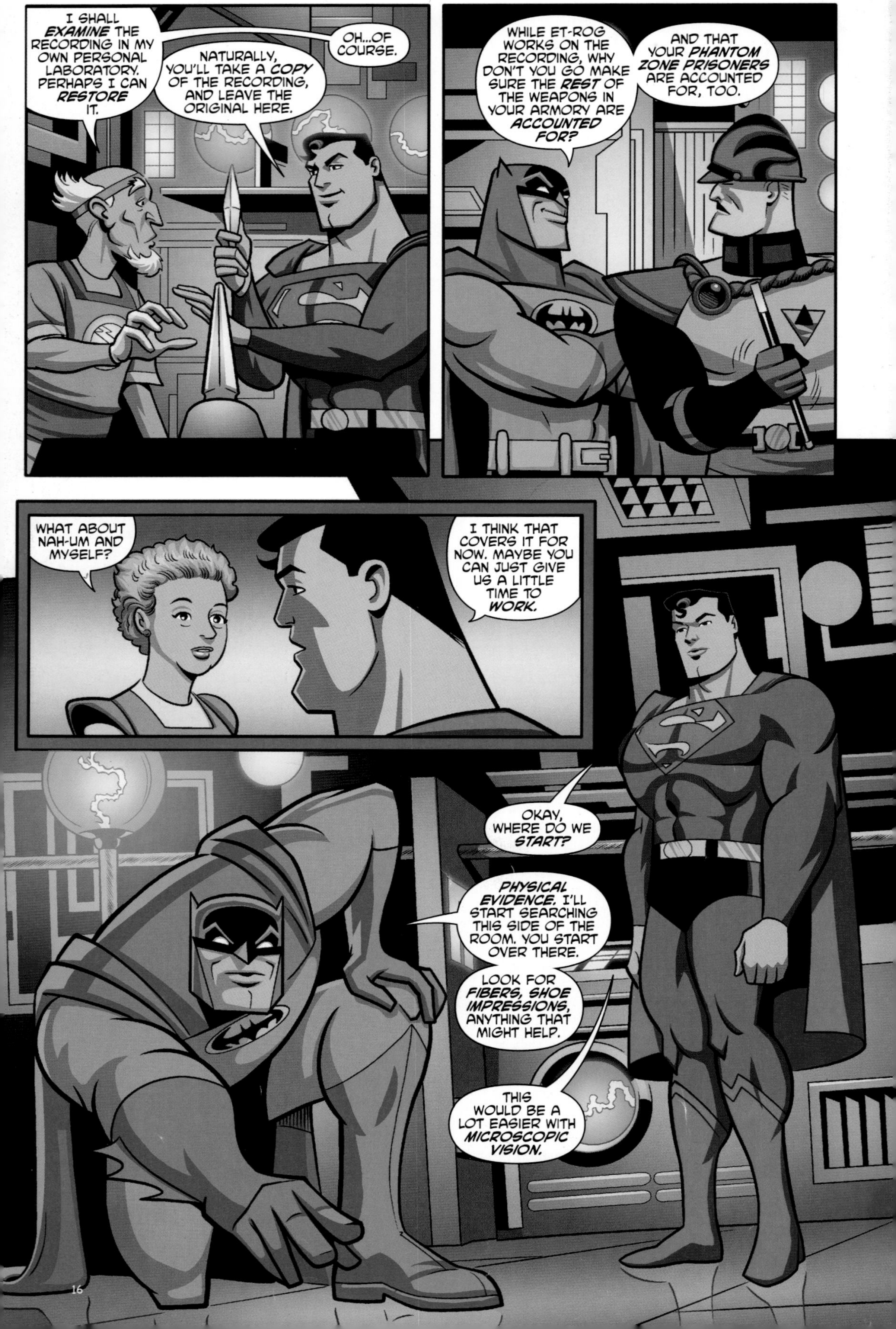
I SHALL EXAMINE THE RECORDING IN MY OWN PERSONAL LABORATORY. PERHAPS I CAN RESTORE IT.
NATURALLY, YOU'LL TAKE A COPY OF THE RECORDING, AND LEAVE THE ORIGINAL HERE.
OH...OF COURSE.
WHILE ET-ROG WORKS ON THE RECORDING, WHY DON'T YOU GO MAKE SURE THE REST OF THE WEAPONS IN YOUR ARMORY ARE ACCOUNTED FOR?
AND THAT YOUR PHANTOM ZONE PRISONERS ARE ACCOUNTED FOR, TOO.
WHAT ABOUT NAH-UM AND MYSELF?
I THINK THAT COVERS IT FOR NOW. MAYBE YOU CAN JUST GIVE US A LITTLE TIME TO WORK.
OKAY, WHERE DO WE START?
PHYSICAL EVIDENCE. I'LL START SEARCHING THIS SIDE OF THE ROOM. YOU START OVER THERE.
LOOK FOR FIBERS, SHOE IMPRESSIONS, ANYTHING THAT MIGHT HELP.
THIS WOULD BE A LOT EASIER WITH MICROSCOPIC VISION.

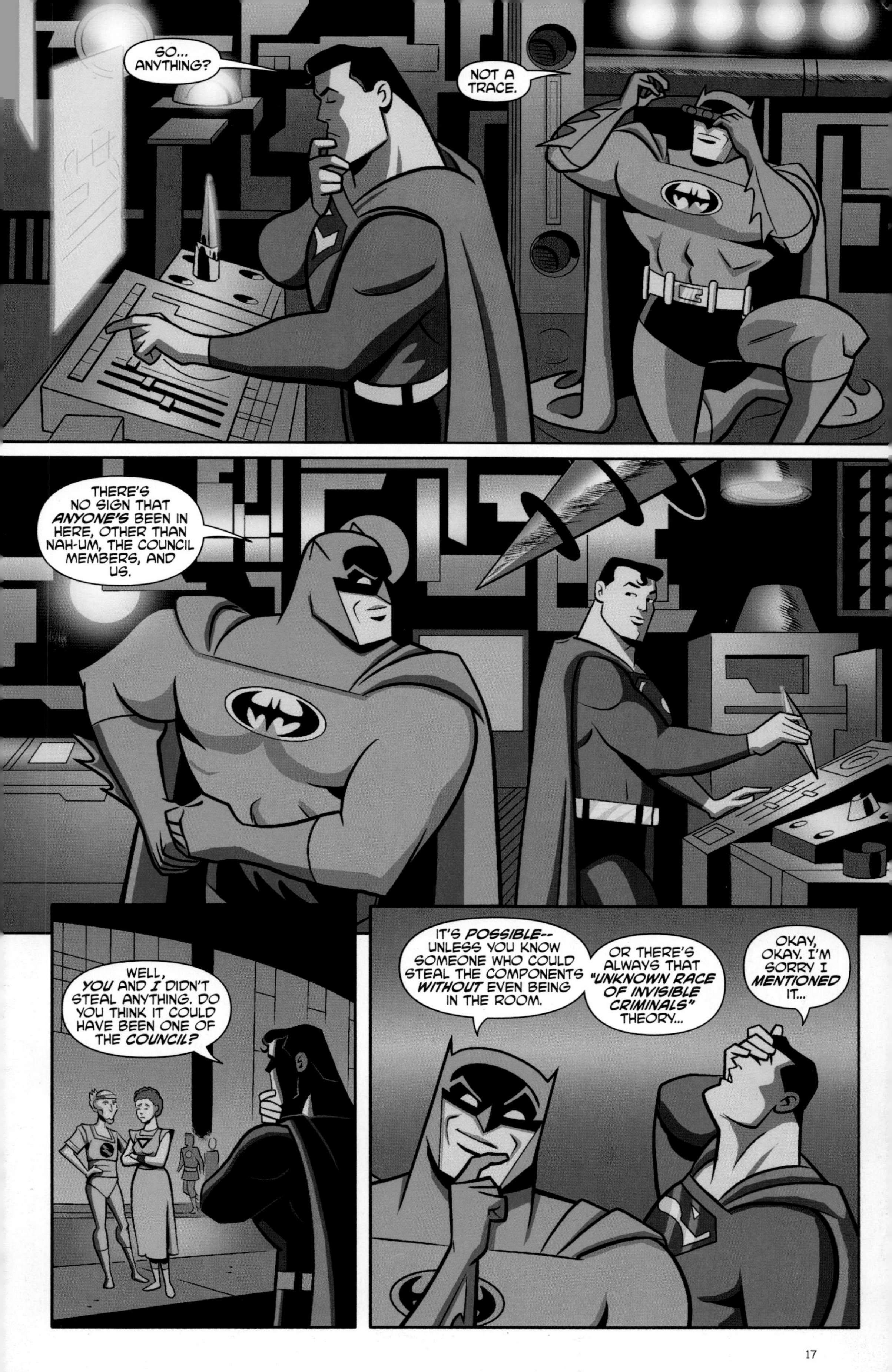
SO... ANYTHING?
NOT A TRACE.
THERE'S NO SIGN THAT ANYONE'S BEEN IN HERE, OTHER THAN NAH-UM, THE COUNCIL MEMBERS, AND US.
WELL, YOU AND I DIDN'T STEAL ANYTHING. DO YOU THINK IT COULD HAVE BEEN ONE OF THE COUNCIL?
IT'S POSSIBLE-- UNLESS YOU KNOW SOMEONE WHO COULD STEAL THE COMPONENTS WITHOUT EVEN BEING IN THE ROOM.
OR THERE'S ALWAYS THAT "UNKNOWN RACE OF INVISIBLE CRIMINALS" THEORY...
OKAY, OKAY. I'M SORRY I MENTIONED IT...

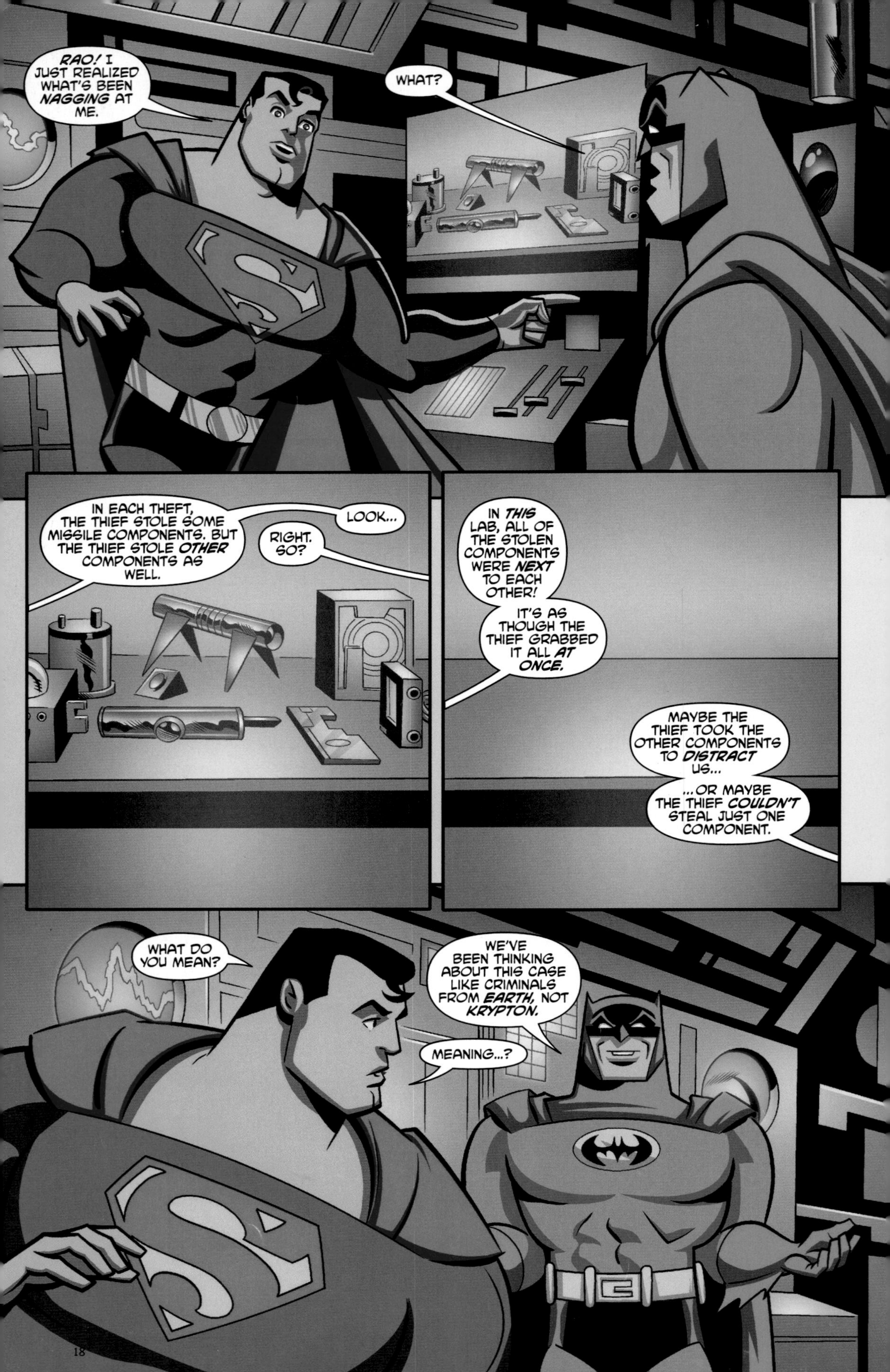

RAO! I JUST REALIZED WHAT'S BEEN NAGGING AT ME.
WHAT?
LOOK...
IN EACH THEFT, THE THIEF STOLE SOME MISSILE COMPONENTS. BUT THE THIEF STOLE OTHER COMPONENTS AS WELL.
RIGHT. SO?
IN THIS LAB, ALL OF THE STOLEN COMPONENTS WERE NEXT TO EACH OTHER!
IT'S AS THOUGH THE THIEF GRABBED IT ALL AT ONCE.
MAYBE THE THIEF TOOK THE OTHER COMPONENTS TO DISTRACT US...
...OR MAYBE THE THIEF COULDN'T STEAL JUST ONE COMPONENT.
WHAT DO YOU MEAN?
WE'VE BEEN THINKING ABOUT THIS CASE LIKE CRIMINALS FROM EARTH, NOT KRYPTON.
MEANING...?

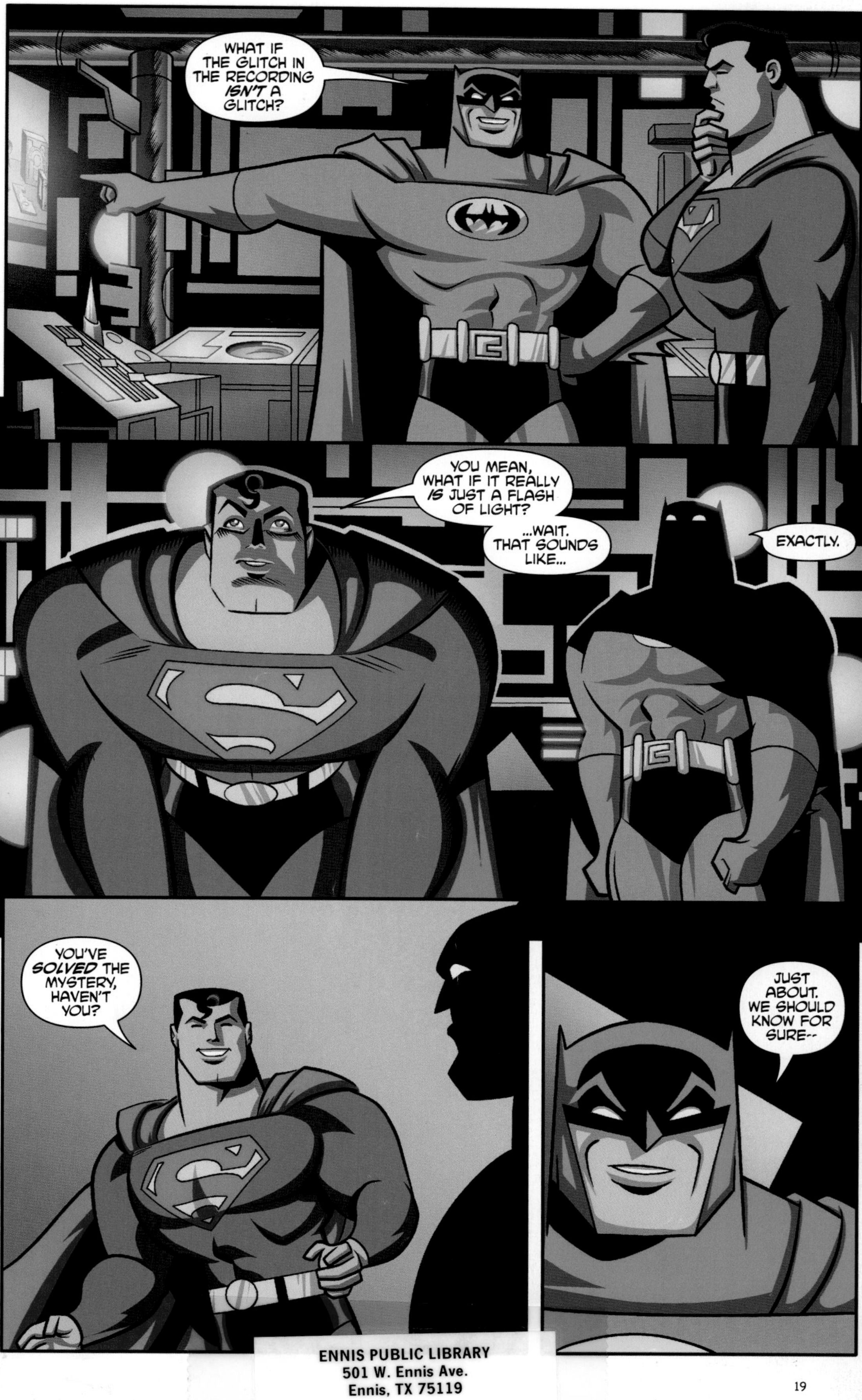
WHAT IF THE GLITCH IN THE RECORDING *ISN'T* A GLITCH?
YOU MEAN, WHAT IF IT REALLY *IS* JUST A FLASH OF LIGHT?
...WAIT. THAT SOUNDS LIKE...
EXACTLY.
YOU'VE *SOLVED* THE MYSTERY, HAVEN'T YOU?
JUST ABOUT. WE SHOULD KNOW FOR SURE--

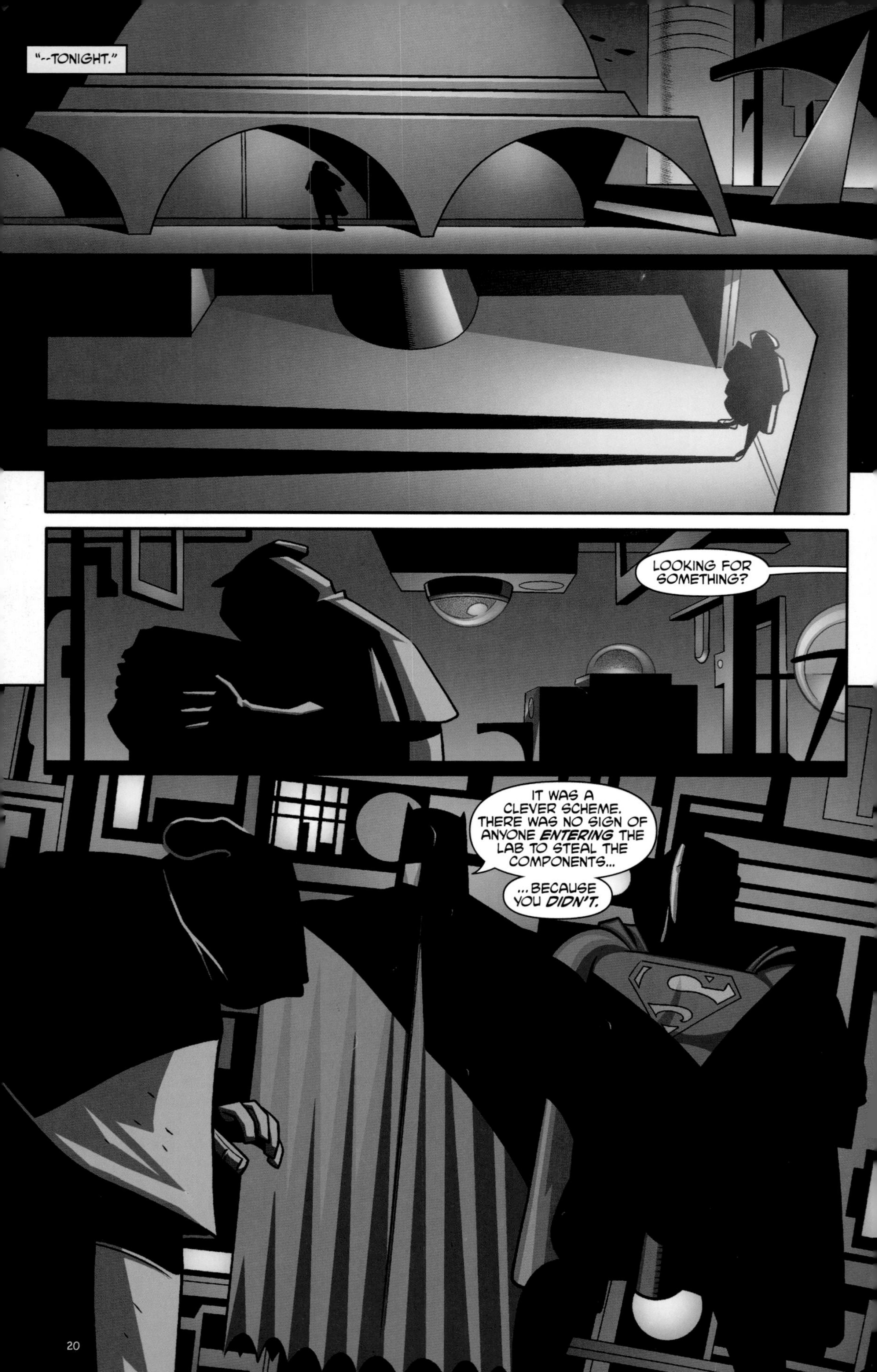
"--TONIGHT."
LOOKING FOR SOMETHING?
IT WAS A CLEVER SCHEME. THERE WAS NO SIGN OF ANYONE *ENTERING* THE LAB TO STEAL THE COMPONENTS...
...BECAUSE YOU *DIDN'T.*

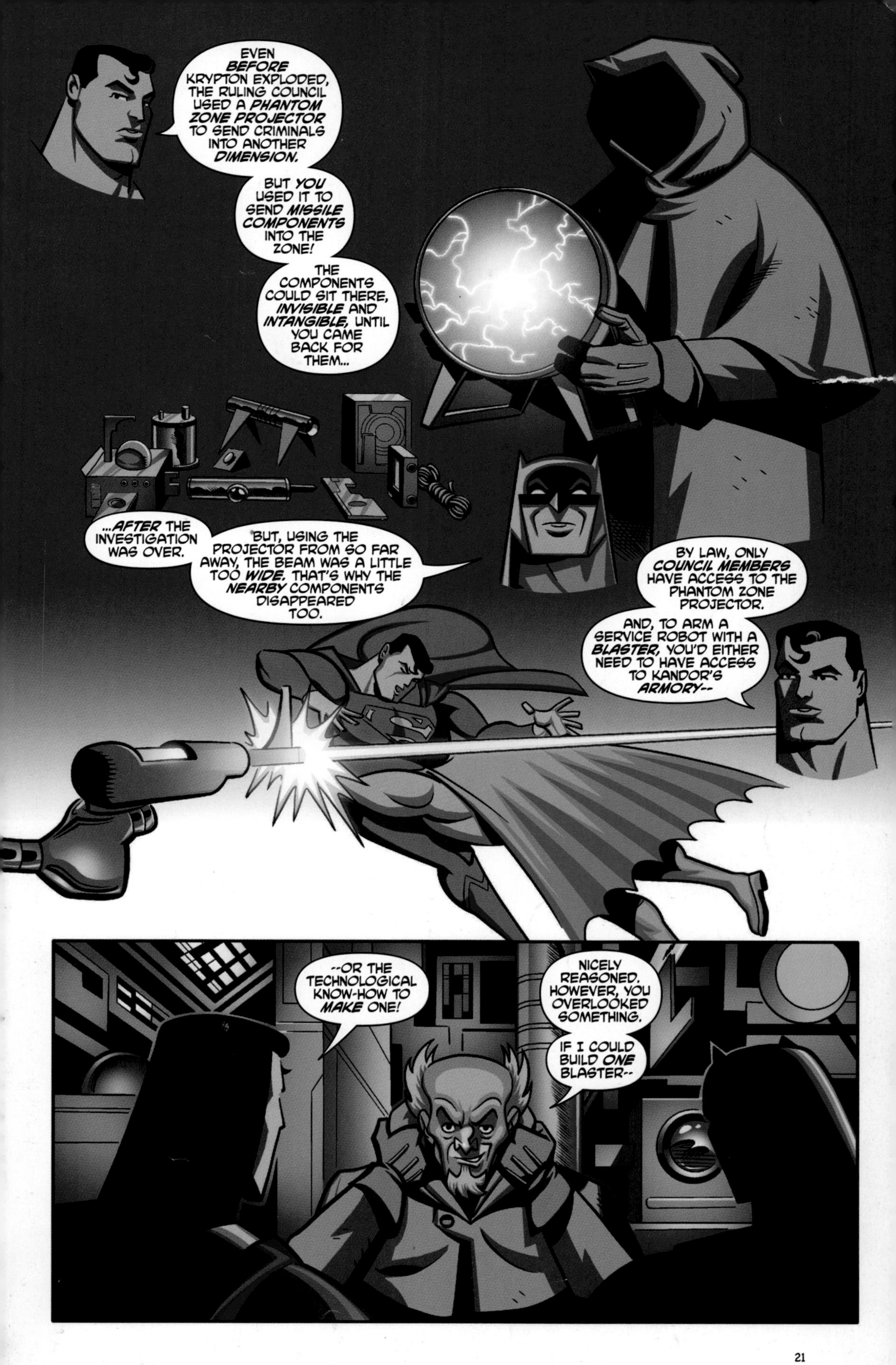
EVEN BEFORE KRYPTON EXPLODED, THE RULING COUNCIL USED A PHANTOM ZONE PROJECTOR TO SEND CRIMINALS INTO ANOTHER DIMENSION.
BUT YOU USED IT TO SEND MISSILE COMPONENTS INTO THE ZONE!
THE COMPONENTS COULD SIT THERE, INVISIBLE AND INTANGIBLE, UNTIL YOU CAME BACK FOR THEM...
...AFTER THE INVESTIGATION WAS OVER.
BUT, USING THE PROJECTOR FROM SO FAR AWAY, THE BEAM WAS A LITTLE TOO WIDE. THAT'S WHY THE NEARBY COMPONENTS DISAPPEARED TOO.
BY LAW, ONLY COUNCIL MEMBERS HAVE ACCESS TO THE PHANTOM ZONE PROJECTOR.
AND, TO ARM A SERVICE ROBOT WITH A BLASTER, YOU'D EITHER NEED TO HAVE ACCESS TO KANDOR'S ARMORY--
--OR THE TECHNOLOGICAL KNOW-HOW TO MAKE ONE!
NICELY REASONED. HOWEVER, YOU OVERLOOKED SOMETHING.
IF I COULD BUILD ONE BLASTER--

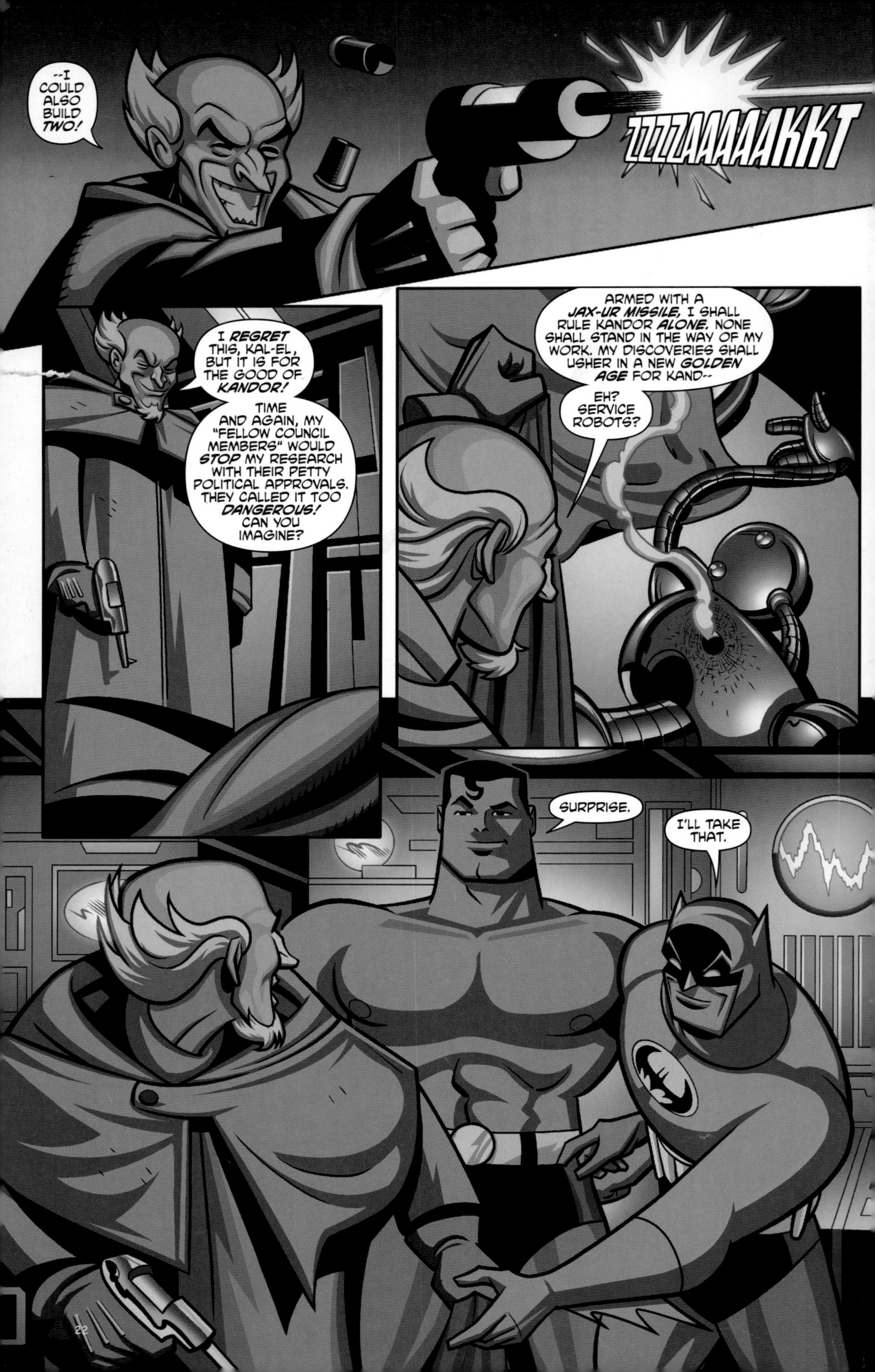
--I COULD ALSO BUILD TWO!
ZZZZAAAAAKKT
I REGRET THIS, KAL-EL, BUT IT IS FOR THE GOOD OF KANDOR!
TIME AND AGAIN, MY "FELLOW COUNCIL MEMBERS" WOULD STOP MY RESEARCH WITH THEIR PETTY POLITICAL APPROVALS. THEY CALLED IT TOO DANGEROUS! CAN YOU IMAGINE?
ARMED WITH A JAX-UR MISSILE, I SHALL RULE KANDOR ALONE. NONE SHALL STAND IN THE WAY OF MY WORK. MY DISCOVERIES SHALL USHER IN A NEW GOLDEN AGE FOR KAND--
EH? SERVICE ROBOTS?
SURPRISE.
I'LL TAKE THAT.

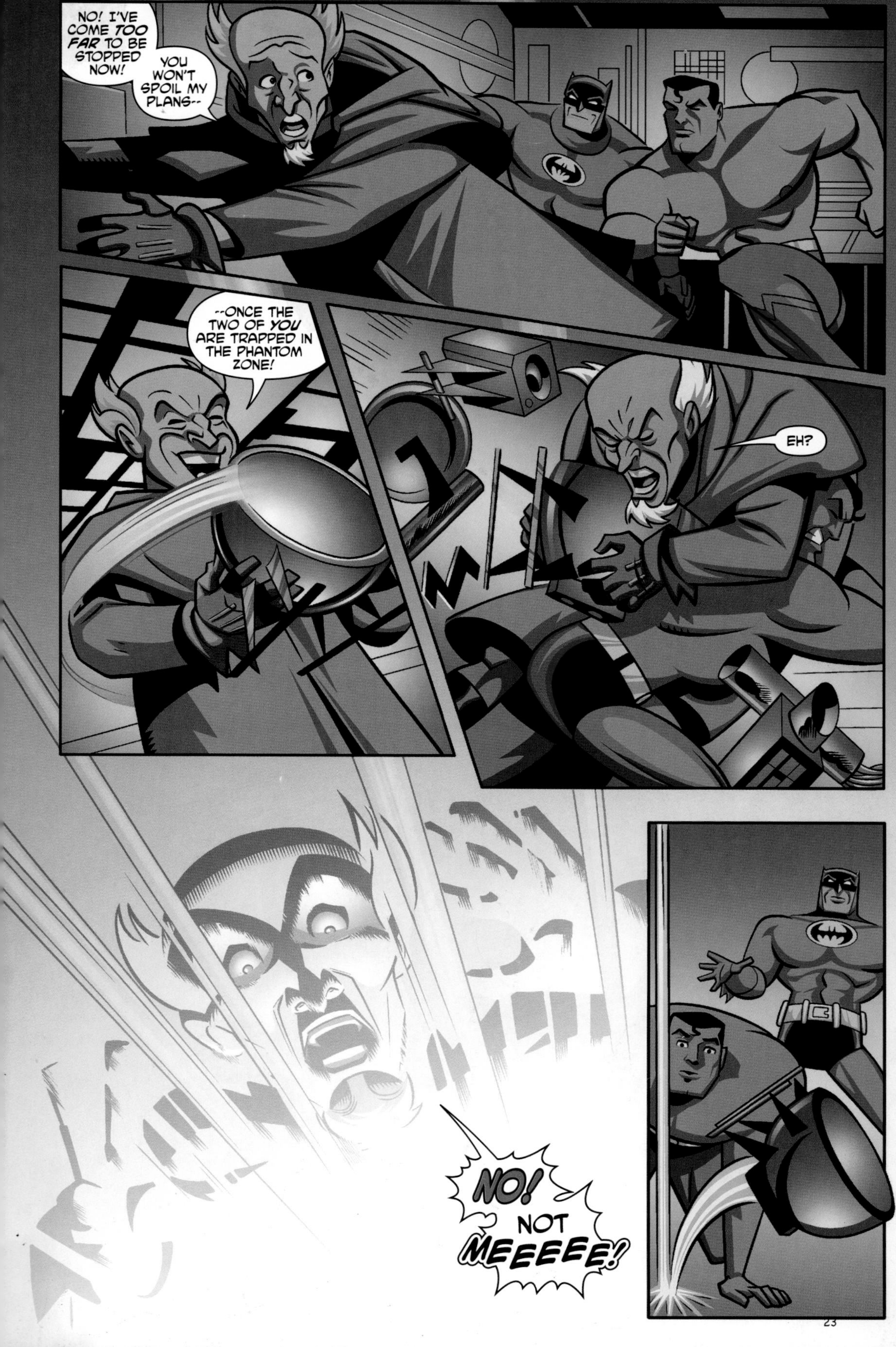
NO! I'VE COME TOO FAR TO BE STOPPED NOW!
YOU WON'T SPOIL MY PLANS--
--ONCE THE TWO OF YOU ARE TRAPPED IN THE PHANTOM ZONE!
EH?
NO! NOT MEEEEE!

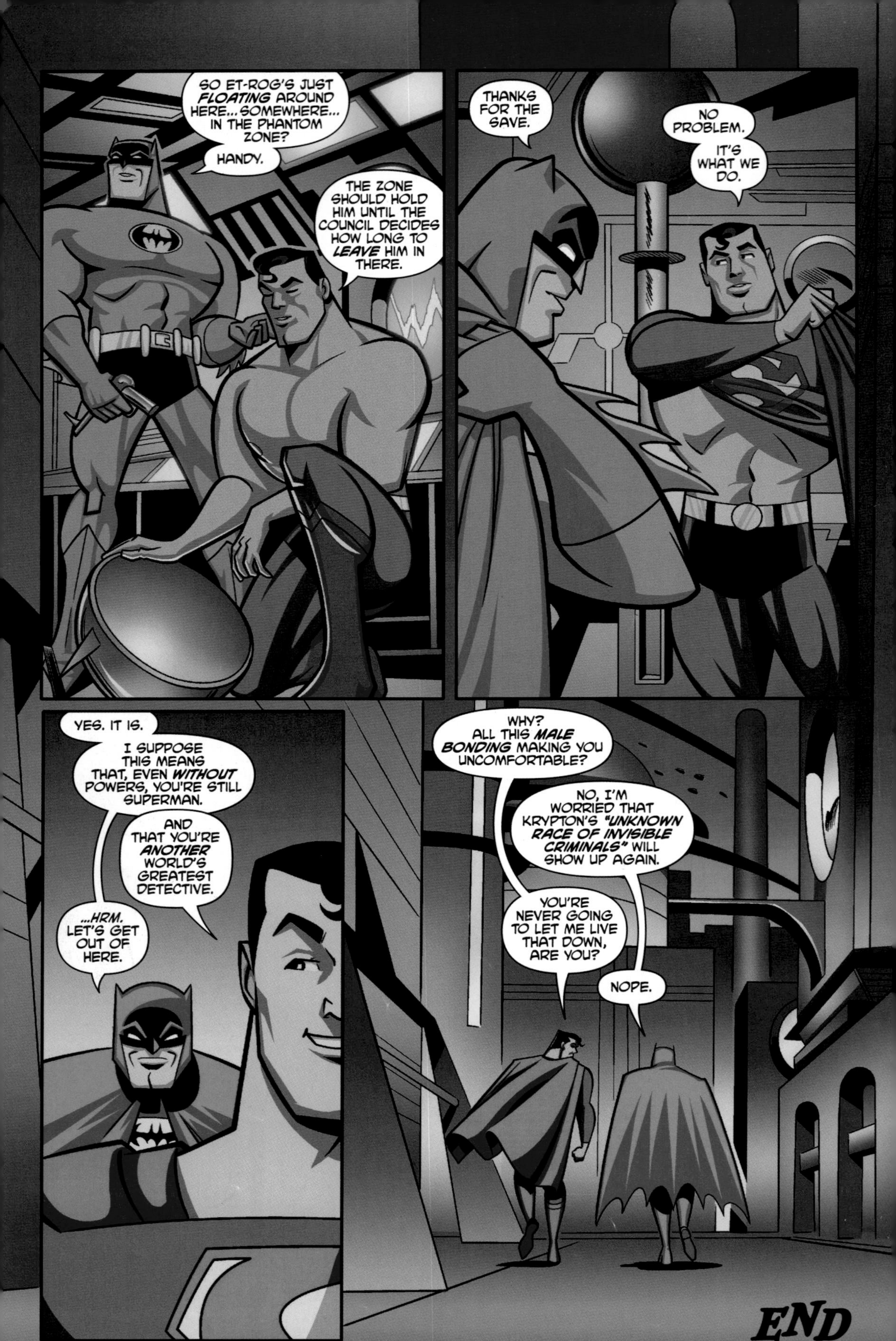
SO ET-ROG'S JUST FLOATING AROUND HERE... SOMEWHERE... IN THE PHANTOM ZONE?
HANDY.
THE ZONE SHOULD HOLD HIM UNTIL THE COUNCIL DECIDES HOW LONG TO LEAVE HIM IN THERE.
THANKS FOR THE SAVE.
NO PROBLEM.
IT'S WHAT WE DO.
YES. IT IS.
I SUPPOSE THIS MEANS THAT, EVEN WITHOUT POWERS, YOU'RE STILL SUPERMAN.
AND THAT YOU'RE ANOTHER WORLD'S GREATEST DETECTIVE.
...HRM. LET'S GET OUT OF HERE.
WHY? ALL THIS MALE BONDING MAKING YOU UNCOMFORTABLE?
NO, I'M WORRIED THAT KRYPTON'S "UNKNOWN RACE OF INVISIBLE CRIMINALS" WILL SHOW UP AGAIN.
YOU'RE NEVER GOING TO LET ME LIVE THAT DOWN, ARE YOU?
NOPE.
END

CREATORS

SHOLLY FISCH
WRITER

Bitten by a radioactive typewriter, Sholly Fisch has spent the wee hours writing books, comics, TV scripts, and online material for over 25 years. His comic book credits include more than 200 stories and features about characters such as Batman, Superman, Bugs Bunny, Daffy Duck, Spider-Man, and Ben 10. Currently, he writes stories for Action Comics every month, plus stories for Looney Tunes and Scooby-Doo. By day, Sholly is a mild-mannered developmental psychologist who helps to create educational TV shows, websites, and other media for kids.

RICK BURCHETT
PENCILLER

Rick Burchett has worked as a comics artist for over 25 years. He has received the comics industry's Eisner Award three times, Spain's Haxtur Award, and he has been nominated for England's Eagle Award. Rick lives with his wife and two sons near St. Louis, Missouri.

DAN DAVIS
INKER

Dan Davis has illustrated the Garfield comic series as well as books for Warner Bros. and DC Comics. He has brought a variety of comic book characters to life, including Batman and the rest of the Super Friends! In 2012, Dan was nominated for an Eisner Award for the Batman: The Brave and the Bold series. He currently resides in Gotham City.

GLOSSARY

artillery [ahr·TIL·ur·ee]--large, powerful guns that are mounted on wheels or tracks

colleagues [KAH·leegz]--people who work with you

complement [KAHM·pluh·muhnt]--to complete something

component [kuhm·POH·nuhnt]--a part of a larger whole

customs [KUHSS·tuhmz]--traditions

dean [DEEN]--the senior member of a group

guild [GILD]--a group of people who have similar interests

intangible [in·TAN·ja·buhl]--impossible to touch

lunatic [LOO·nuh·tik]--someone who is insane or who behaves foolishly

malfunction [mal·FUHNK·shuhn]--to fail to operate properly

rash [RASH]--an occurrence of many events of the same type

technological [tek·nuh·LAH·ji·kuhl]--related to science or engineering

unconscious [uhn·KAHN·shuhs]--not awake; unable to see, feel, or think

VISUAL QUESTIONS & PROMPTS

1. Batman and Superman teamed up to solve this case. How did they work together? What were each of their strengths?

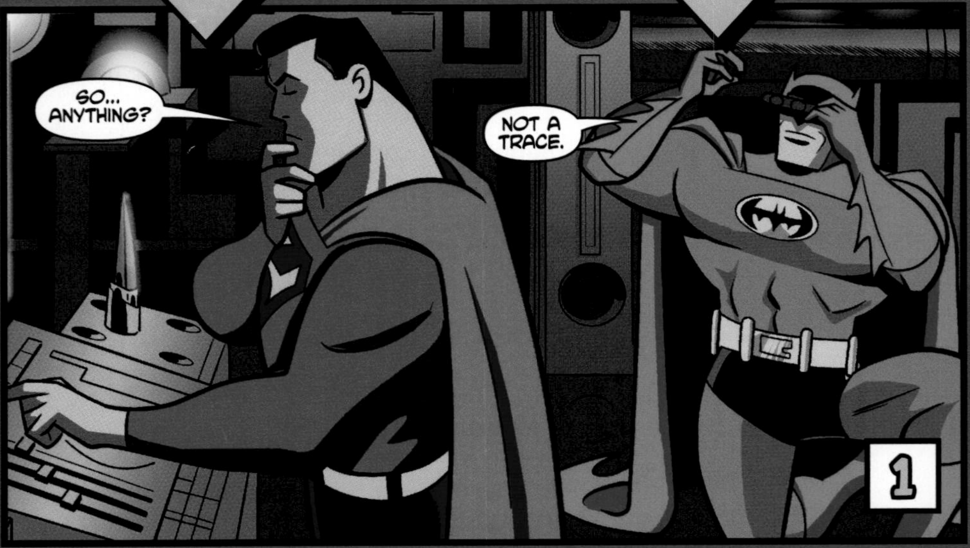
SO... ANYTHING?
NOT A TRACE.
1

2. What about this frame indicates that it's a memory? How do you know?

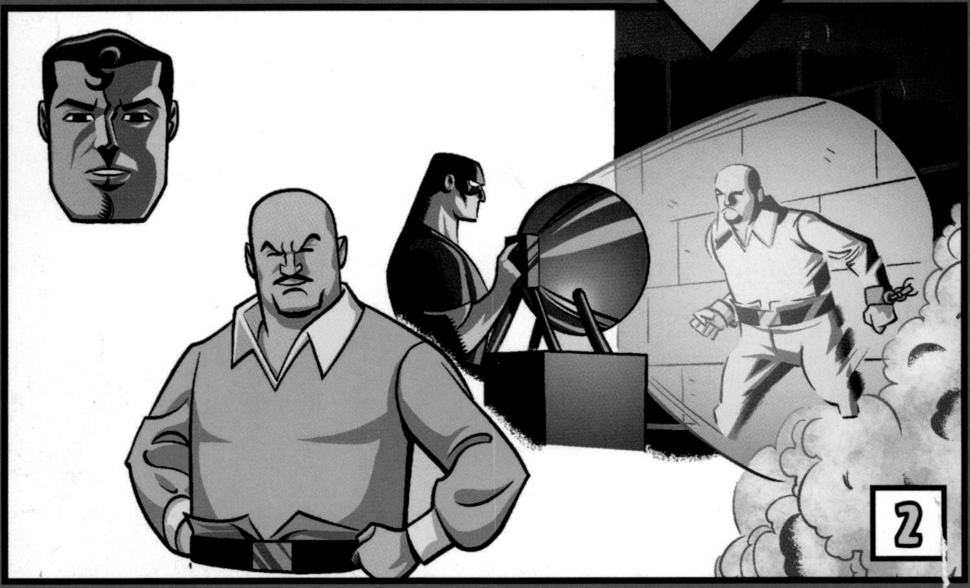
2

3. How do you think thieves on Krypton might be different from thieves on Earth?

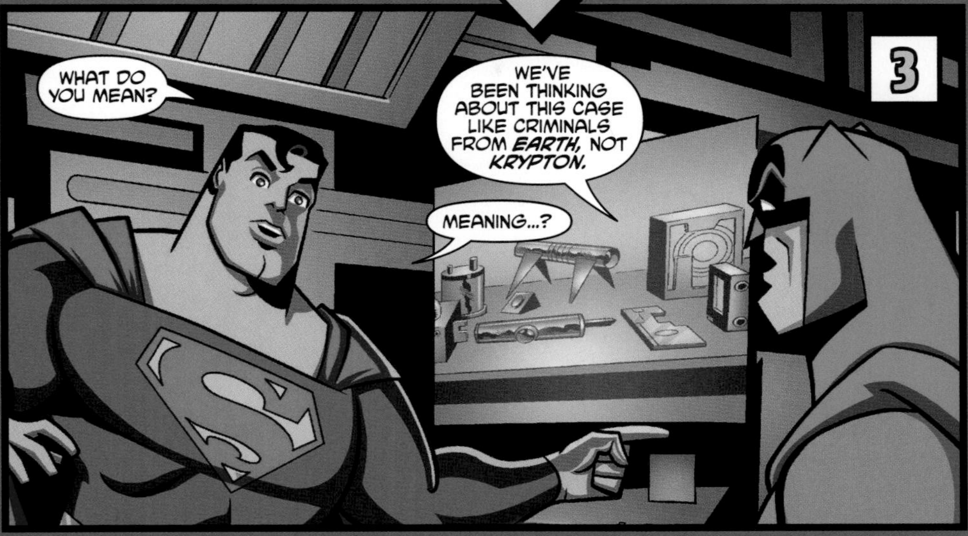
3
WHAT DO YOU MEAN?
WE'VE BEEN THINKING ABOUT THIS CASE LIKE CRIMINALS FROM *EARTH,* NOT *KRYPTON.*
MEANING...?

4. Why do you think the artists chose to make the whole panel dark except for the emblem on Superman's chest? What, if anything, do you think the effect adds to the story?

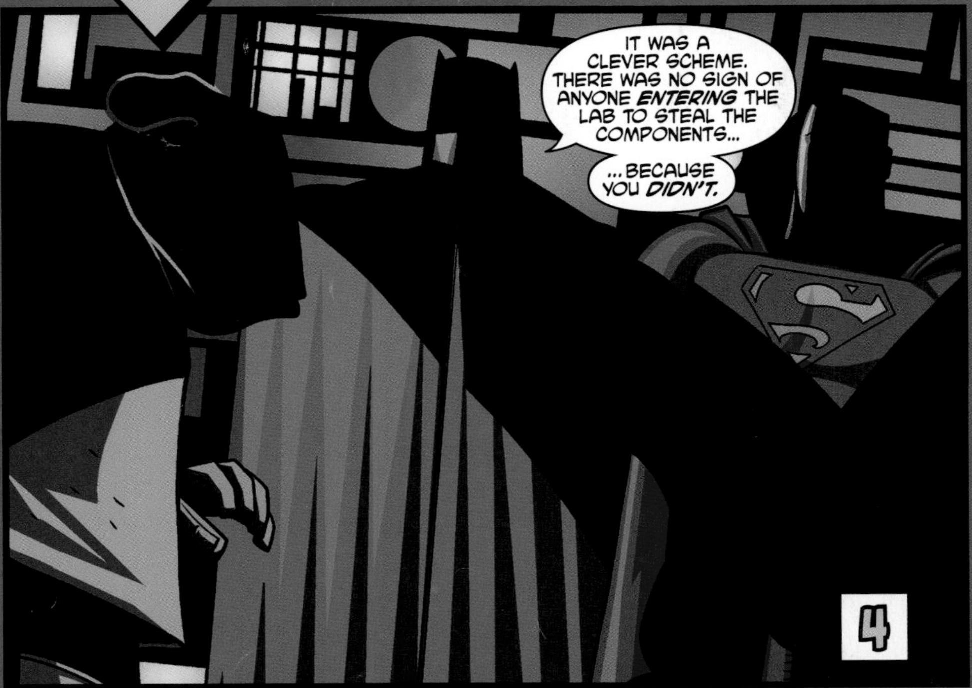
IT WAS A CLEVER SCHEME. THERE WAS NO SIGN OF ANYONE *ENTERING* THE LAB TO STEAL THE COMPONENTS...
...BECAUSE YOU *DIDN'T.*
4

READ THEM ALL!

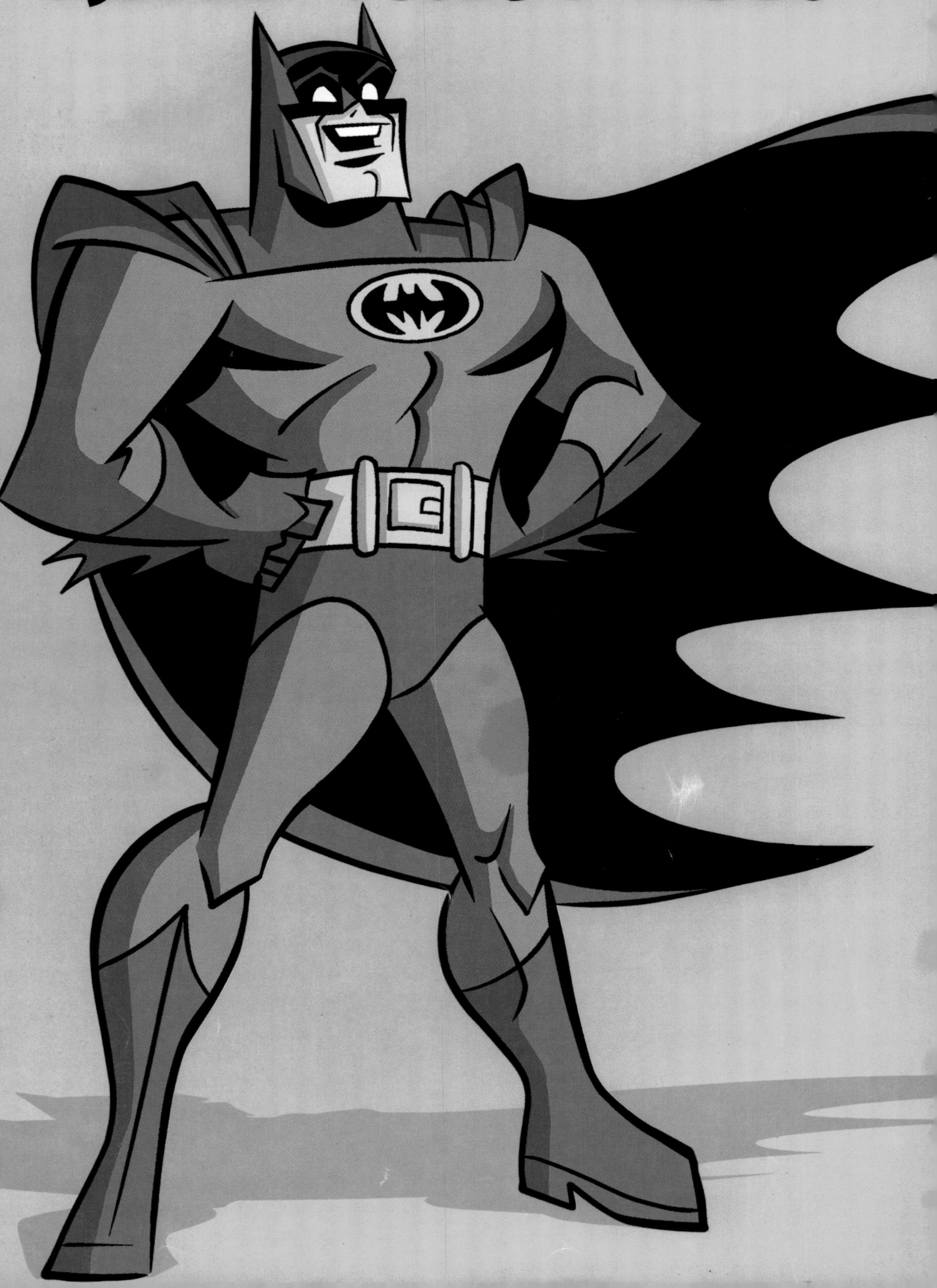

THE ALL NEW!

BATMAN

THE BRAVE AND THE BOLD

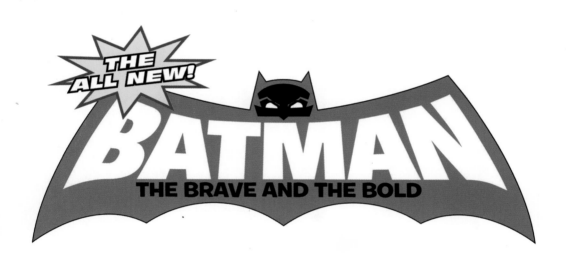

THE ALL NEW! BATMAN
THE BRAVE AND THE BOLD

THE ALL NEW!
BATMAN
THE BRAVE AND THE BOLD
BATTLE OF THE PLANETS
FISCH
BURCHETT
DAVIS

THE ALL NEW!
BATMAN
THE BRAVE AND THE BOLD
THAT HOLIDAY FEELING
FISCH
BURCHETT
DAVIS

THE ALL NEW!
BATMAN
THE BRAVE AND THE BOLD
THROUGH THE LOOKING GLASS
FISCH
BURCHETT
DAVIS

THE ALL NEW!
BATMAN
THE BRAVE AND THE BOLD
FISCH
BURCHETT
DAVIS
THE BRIDE AND THE BOLD

THE ALL NEW!
BATMAN
THE BRAVE AND THE BOLD
FISCH
BURCHETT
DAVIS
MANHANDLED BY MANHUNTERS!

THE ALL NEW!
BATMAN
THE BRAVE AND THE BOLD
FISCH
BURCHETT
DAVIS
CLOBBERED BY CLAYFACE!

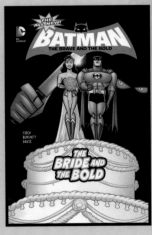

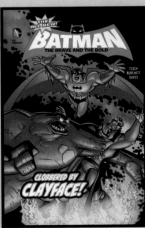

2/13/15